"The last thing someone like you needs in her life is someone like me."

"Thanks for the warning."

Courtney turned her small boat toward the cove. She wouldn't leave herself open and vulnerable around Blair again. She deserved complete honesty, and that was what he'd given her. If it hurt, so be it. Better to be hurt now, before this went any further.

As he tossed the anchor over the side, they started toward the dock. Blair put a hand on her arm and pointed.

A thin ribbon of light was moving around the perimeter of his cottage. He motioned for her to remain behind while he hurried ashore.

Courtney dashed through the shallows and reached shore just behind Blair. At the sound of their splashing, the light was extinguished. All that could be seen was a shadowy figure dissolving into the darkness. The only sound was hurried footsteps receding into the distance.

Then there was only silence, but for the gentle lap of water against the shore.

Dear Reader,

Welcome to another month of excitingly romantic reading from Silhouette Intimate Moments. Ruth Langan starts things off with a bang in *Vendetta,* the third of her four DEVIL'S COVE titles. Blair Colby came back to town looking for a quiet summer. Instead he found danger, mystery—and love.

Fans of Sara Orwig's STALLION PASS miniseries will be glad to see it continued in *Bring On The Night,* part of STALLION PASS: TEXAS KNIGHTS, also a fixture in Silhouette Desire. Mix one tough agent, the ex-wife he's never forgotten and the son he never knew existed, and you have a recipe for high emotion. Whether you experienced our FAMILY SECRETS continuity or are new to it now, you won't want to miss our six FAMILY SECRETS: THE NEXT GENERATION titles, starting with Jenna Mills' *A Cry In The Dark.* Ana Leigh's *Face of Deception* is the first of her BISHOP'S HEROES stories, and your heart will beat faster with every step of Mike Bishop's mission to rescue Ann Hamilton and her adopted son from danger. Are you a fan of the paranormal? Don't miss *One Eye Open,* popular author Karen Whiddon's first book for the line, which features a shape-shifting heroine and a hero who's all man. Finally, go *To The Limit* with new author Virginia Kelly, who really knows how to write heart-pounding romantic adventure.

And come back next month, for more of the best and most exciting romance reading around, right here in Silhouette Intimate Moments.

Yours,

Leslie J. Wainger
Executive Editor

Please address questions and book requests to:
Silhouette Reader Service
U.S.: 3010 Walden Ave., P.O. Box 1325, Buffalo, NY 14269
Canadian: P.O. Box 609, Fort Erie, Ont. L2A 5X3

RUTH LANGAN
Vendetta

Silhouette®

INTIMATE MOMENTS™

Published by Silhouette Books

America's Publisher of Contemporary Romance

SILHOUETTE BOOKS

ISBN 0-373-27367-3

VENDETTA

Copyright © 2004 by Ruth Ryan Langan

This edition published by arrangement with Harlequin Books S.A.

® and TM are trademarks of Harlequin Books S.A., used under license.
Trademarks indicated with ® are registered in the United States Patent
and Trademark Office, the Canadian Trade Marks Office and in other
countries.

Visit Silhouette Books at www.eHarlequin.com

Printed in U.S.A.

Books by Ruth Langan

RUTH LANGAN

is an award-winning and bestselling author. Her books have been finalists for the Romance Writers of America's (RWA) RITA® Award. Over the years, she has given dozens of print, radio and TV interviews, including *Good Morning America* and *CNN News,* and has been quoted in such diverse publications as the *Wall Street Journal, Cosmopolitan* and the *Detroit Free Press.* Married to her childhood sweetheart, she has raised five children and lives in Michigan, the state where she was born and raised. Ruth enjoys hearing from her readers. Letters can be sent via e-mail to ryanlangan@aol.com or via her Web site at www.ryanlangan.com.

For our very own Courtney Langan, lucky number 20.
I hope you dance.

And for Tom,
who brought me to the dance.

My special thanks to Haley and Kelsey Bissonnette,
for sharing with me their valuable experience in sailing.

Prologue

Devil's Cove, Michigan—2003

Retired judge Frank Brennan had just taken a turn around the gardens of his lovely old home known as The Willows. With a sigh of satisfaction he settled himself in his favorite leather chair in his office. His wife, Bert, had already retired for the night, and he'd promised to join her upstairs in a few minutes.

When the phone rang he picked it up absently. "Hello."

"Poppie?" At the strangled voice of his granddaughter on the other end of the line, the old man sat up straighter, cupping the phone in both hands.

"Courtney?"

"Oh, Poppie. I had to talk to you."

He knew by the way her voice trembled that she was fighting tears. That in itself was difficult to imagine, since he'd always seen Courtney, the third of his son Christopher's daughters, as the strongest of his grandchildren. Courtney, who had decided while still in high school that she wanted to study interior design, and had never veered from her charted course. Courtney, who had graduated from the prestigious New York School of Design before going on to Paris and then Rome, before settling in Milan, where she had opened a lovely studio and boutique with her partner, Pietro Amalfi.

"What's wrong, sweetheart?"

He heard her take a deep breath. "It's Pietro. He…" She struggled to get the words out over the tears that had started up again. "I found out that he's been…stealing. None of the bills have been paid. And now the bank is threatening to take our shop. And that's not all. He's run off with—" she paused before managing to say "—with one of the girls I'd hired in the boutique."

Frank Brennan listened in silence as the story

poured out. It was a tale as old as time, but one that never got easier to hear, especially when it broke the heart of someone as dear as this beautiful young woman, who had been wildly in love for the first time in her life.

When the words had all been said, and the only sounds were an occasional hiccupping sob, Frank's tone gentled. ''You asked me what I think, so I'll tell you. I think you need to come home, honey. To be with the people who love you.''

''But I feel like such a fool. If I run home now, I'll look like a failure, as well, Poppie.''

''When it comes to affairs of the heart, Courtney my love, we're all fools. But a failure? Never. If it would make matters simpler, I can recommend a good law firm in Milan to handle this sad affair. Once Pietro is apprehended, he will be ordered to make restitution or go to jail.''

''I don't want to send him to jail, Poppie. I just want my credit cleared and a chance to start over.''

''One thing at a time, Courtney. Pietro may have mishandled your heart and your business, but he can't be allowed to walk away without paying a price. After that, you can move ahead with your life.''

After a strained silence she gave a long, deep sigh. "I know you're right, Poppie. Thank you. I'll contact the law firm. Maybe once I get things started, I'll be able to think more clearly."

"Good girl. And when this is behind you, you need to come home. I can't think of anything better for your heart and soul than to spend a summer here at The Willows while you plan your future."

There was a long pause before she said simply, "I knew I could count on you to say just the right thing. I'll be home as soon as I've dealt with this."

When he replaced the receiver, Frank reached across the desk and picked up a framed photograph taken more than fifteen years earlier. In it, four little girls stood with their arms around each other. Emily was clutching one of her many stray kittens. Hannah's knees were grass-stained from weeding the garden. Sidney was holding one of her drawings, and her nose and cheek were streaked with finger paint. Courtney's tennis shorts and shirt looked as crisp and white as when she'd put them on hours earlier. Her waist-length caramel hair was plaited in two perfect braids. Her dimpled smile was angelic.

Frank thought of the callous young man who had just broken her trust and her heart. Knowing his tough, perfectionist granddaughter, she would build a shield around that heart to keep it from being hurt again. It would take a long time, if ever, for her to trust another man.

He whispered a prayer that somewhere in this world there was not only one worthy of that fine heart but wise enough to break through the defenses she would surely build as strong, as high, as any fortress.

Chapter 1

Devil's Cove—Present Day

"Poppie? Got a minute?"

At the sound of Courtney's voice, Frank Brennan tore his attention from the legal journal he'd been reading and looked up with a smile. "I always have time for one of my favorite granddaughters." Since he referred to all four of his granddaughters as his favorite, Courtney merely chuckled.

He indicated the chair across from his desk in his office. Though he'd been retired from the law for a decade, he continued to fill his days, when he wasn't gardening, in his favorite room poring over the latest legal cases, especially those involving his home district. ''What's on your mind, my darling?''

''I was talking to Bert about the Colby cottage.''

Just the mention of his wife, Alberta, whom everyone called Bert, had his smile widening. ''Bert knew Sarah Colby better than I did. A private woman. Kept to herself. Never married, and as far as I know, had little family.''

''I was thinking, now that she's gone, that I might try to buy the place.''

Frank felt a quickening of his heartbeat. Since Courtney had returned to Devil's Cove more than a year ago, he'd been holding his breath, hoping she might consider staying, but trying to resign himself that she might soon hunger for the exotic life she'd left behind. ''Sounds like a commitment.''

She laughed. ''I guess it does. I love my apartment above the shop, but if I could move into the Colby cottage, I'd have twice the space. Plus I could add a stone walkway between the two buildings, and gardens to display the garden art I've been accumulating.''

She had given this a good deal of thought, he could see. "It makes sense from a business standpoint. Since the two buildings share a driveway, and the cottage is directly behind your shop, most folks would probably mistake it as one address and one owner, anyway."

Courtney nodded. "That's what I think, too. Bert said she remembers a nephew at the funeral, but she heard that he'd taken a big job out of the country. I checked with the city clerk, and she said a law firm in Boston is handling Sarah's estate. I'd like your help drafting a letter to the firm asking if the cottage is for sale, and whether or not they would consider my offer to purchase."

Frank reached into his drawer and withdrew a legal tablet. "Write down what you just said, and I'll add the proper language before we have the document drawn up for your signature."

Courtney rounded the desk and pressed a kiss to his cheek. "What would I do without you, Poppie?"

He chuckled. "Let's hope you don't have to find out for many a year, my darling."

"It has to be something really unique." Prentice Osborn took another turn around Courtney Brennan's gift shop, Treasures. "I want to give it to Carrie tonight when I ask her—'' He stopped abruptly when he realized what he'd almost revealed and glanced over quickly at the only other patron in the shop, Wade Bentley, the mayor of Devil's Cove, who was being assisted by Kendra Crowley, the high-school graduate Courtney had hired to help in the shop for the summer. The mayor seemed to be busy examining a display of pretty painted glassware on the far side of the room. ''Not a word, Courtney.''

''My lips are sealed.'' Though she didn't crack a smile, the glint of humor in Courtney's eyes gave her away. The romance between Prentice, who belonged to one of Devil's Cove's wealthiest families and Carrie Lester, who worked in the Daisy Diner, was the worst-kept secret in town. It was impossible not to notice Prentice hanging around the diner for hours while Carrie worked her shift, just so he could walk her home.

At first, whenever they went out to dinner, they'd taken along his mentally-challenged brother Will and Carrie's daughter Jenny. Lately they'd been seen without their chaperons, lingering over seafood and the world's best cheesecake at The Pier, one of Devil's Cove's finest restaurants.

"How about this?" Courtney held up a hand-painted gargoyle.

"I said unique, not ugly."

"I think it's adorable. Knowing Carrie, she'd agree."

He gave it a closer appraisal. "Do you really think Carrie would like something like that?"

"Absolutely. Look." Courtney held it up to the window. "The artist gave it a secret." Light spilled through, revealing a tiny heart that could only be seen when it was turned a certain way.

"Wow." Prentice took it from Courtney's hand and turned it this way and that, watching the heart appear and disappear. Just looking at it had him grinning.

He seemed to be reconsidering. "It's different, all right. I'm just not sure it's special enough. How will I know if she really likes it, or if she's just humoring me?"

Courtney gave her childhood friend a gentle smile. "Prentice, Carrie is going to love anything you buy for her."

"Is it that obvious?" He actually blushed, a trait that Courtney found endearing.

"It is." She patted his arm. "But your secret is safe with me."

Prentice sighed before handing over the gargoyle. "All right. Wrap it up. I'm going to give it to her tonight after dinner. Right before I ask her...the big question."

Courtney cushioned the little sculpture in tissue before fitting it into one of the gold-and-silver boxes that bore the name Treasures on the lid. That, in turn, was tucked into a handled bag with the same gold-and-silver coin design. The bags had become such a fashion statement, they were the favorite totes of many of the town's tourists and year-round residents.

Courtney handed him his credit card and receipt along with the bag. "Good luck, Prentice."

"Thanks." He paused. "You've got a great shop here, Courtney. I know I'm not the only one in town who's glad you came home. You've added a lot of class to Devil's Cove."

"Thanks, Prentice. Have a good night." She watched as he walked outside, then turned to where the mayor was still studying the glassware.

"See anything you like, Wade?" Courtney glanced at her watch, eager to close up shop. She'd been here since her first delivery at nine, and it was now well past the dinner hour.

The mayor shrugged and ambled toward the counter, carrying a pair of hand-painted candlesticks. "Thinking about buying these. Your young assistant tells me they're all the rage."

"They're beautiful. I don't believe I've ever seen you in Treasures before, Wade."

He smiled, showing white, even teeth in a handsome, tanned face. In his early forties, he still ran the annual summer marathon and routinely beat runners years younger.

The Bentley family had been involved in politics in the state since Wade's father Dade Bentley had been governor. The name alone was enough to guarantee recognition wherever he went. When Wade had decided to make his mark in the city of Devil's Cove, he'd found little competition. There was talk that he might be considering a run for the state senate in the next year. With his family history, his good looks and winning way with people, it was rumored that he might even use that as a stepping stone to Washington.

Courtney began carefully wrapping the candlesticks, before placing them in a bag.

He handed over his charge card. "The city clerk tells me you're interested in buying the Colby cottage."

Courtney smiled. "That's right. I guess there's not much that goes on in this town that you don't know about, Wade."

He returned the smile before signing the sales slip. "Not much. What're you planning on doing with it? Not tearing it down, I hope."

"I'd live there and enlarge my shop, maybe turn the upstairs where I'm living now into an art gallery."

He glanced around. "A fine idea, Courtney. You've got a really nice place here. I guess the Colby cottage would be a nice addition to your holdings." He turned away. "Good night."

"'Night, Wade."

As soon as he was gone, Kendra walked behind the counter and retrieved her denim bag from a locked cabinet. Her hair, bright orange spikes, framed a heart-shaped face made sultry by dark, sooty eyelids and a mouth outlined in deep purple. Kendra bought all her clothes from a nearby resale shop, the more outrageous the better. Today she wore a shapeless fringed sack dress that might have been popular in the seventies, topped by a fitted denim vest painted with old peace signs. She'd confided to Courtney that she was only going on to college in the fall to please her father. Her real goal was to own her own retail shop.

"Geez," she huffed as she slung her bag over her shoulder. "I thought he'd never leave."

"Hey, a sale's a sale. Besides, it doesn't hurt

to have the town's mayor shopping here. And he bought some very expensive candlesticks.''

''Yeah. I'm not complaining. But he took long enough.'' Kendra started toward the door, where her boyfriend, sporting teal, spiked hair and a tie-dyed T-shirt straight out of the sixties, was waiting. ''See you tomorrow.''

''Thanks, Kendra. And thanks for steering the mayor toward that glassware.''

''No problem.''

Courtney followed the young woman to the door and locked it behind her before flipping over the little sign, indicating the time the shop would be opened in the morning. She picked up a clutch of mail before heading for the back room and the stairs that led to her apartment above the shop.

Once there she kicked off her shoes and poured herself an iced tea before sorting through the mail. Except for the usual bills, the letter she'd been hoping for was conspicuously absent.

In the time she'd been back, Courtney had turned this tiny shop into the talk of the town. Though she'd originally intended to stay only long enough to mend her heartache, she'd discovered something about her hometown. There was as much charm in the little town of Devil's Cove as there was in Milan or Paris. And the number of local artists and artisans continued to surprise her. The quality of their workmanship was equal to or better than their European counterparts.

Courtney had never regretted coming home. Though she'd once thought of it as an admission of defeat, she now realized that this town and its people had always held a special place in her heart. The bond she had with her family was stronger than ever. And the thought of being close to her grandparents in their sunset years gave her such pleasure. Not that Bert and Poppie were old. At least, not in Courtney's eyes. Despite their ages, they were the youngest-at-heart people she knew.

She walked to the balcony and looked out at the cottage that stood behind her place. Since Sarah Colby's death, Courtney had begun keeping a close eye on the empty cottage. It saddened her to see no gardens planted. No vines drifting from the window boxes that Sarah had so lovingly painted and planted each year.

The vacant cottage was apparently an object of some interest. Several times Courtney had seen beams of light being played along the darkened building. Fearing vandalism, she'd asked Police Chief Boyd Thompson to dispatch a scout car to the location. Now the police routinely drove by the cottage several times a week.

Courtney wondered how long it would take to hear from the law firm in Boston. Knowing how slowly these things moved through the courts, Courtney couldn't hold back the dreams she'd begun weaving. By moving into the cottage, she could double the space of her shop. And because the property behind the Colby Cottage ran right down to the water's edge, she could keep her boat there. She could already picture the little paved courtyard she was planning between the shop and the cottage, ringed with gardens, which would make the perfect showcase for the garden sculptures she'd begun accumulating from several local artists.

She was just turning away when she caught sight of a shadowy figure darting across the yard. While she watched, the figure paused at the door to the cottage and began turning the knob.

She was across the room in seconds, dashing barefoot down the stairs and across the yard while she dialed the emergency number on her cell phone.

"You, there." She struggled for breath. "Stop right where you are."

The figure, halfway across the threshold, froze,

before turning. At first glance she sucked in a breath. The man facing her was so tall she had to tilt her head to see his eyes. In the moonlight they appeared as icy as the waters of Lake Michigan in winter, and were narrowed on her with a challenging look.

"Is there a problem?" His voice matched his eyes. Frigid. Tinged with arrogance.

"There will be if you try to break in there."

Now she had his full attention.

His tone cooled by degrees. "What business is it of yours where I go?"

"I've been watching out for this property since the owner died."

"I see. And you would be…?"

"Courtney Brennan."

"Brennan?" He looked at her with new interest. "I'm Blair Colby. Sarah's nephew." He picked up a duffel lying near his feet. "I was told by Hibner and Sloan that you contacted them about buying the place."

"Oh." Her relief was evident in the smile that touched her mouth. "You've come to discuss the terms. Would you like to come over to my place and we can talk? That's my shop, and I live above it."

He barely flicked a glance in her direction.

"Sorry to mislead you. I didn't come to sell. I'll be staying here at the cottage, at least for the summer."

"I see." Her heart fell. "Then I'm sorry to have bothered you."

"No bother."

They both looked up as a police cruiser came to a screeching halt and a burly figure in uniform strode toward them.

"Trouble, Courtney?"

"I'm sorry, Boyd. I overreacted. This is Sarah's nephew, Blair Colby. This is our police chief, Boyd Thompson."

"Chief." Blair offered a handshake. "Nice to see everyone is looking out for my aunt's place."

Boyd put his hands on his hips. "You got some ID?"

A flicker of annoyance crossed Blair's face as he once again dropped his duffel before reaching into his back pocket and removing a wallet. Flipping it open he held it up while the police officer studied it in the beam of his flashlight.

"Okay." Boyd nodded. "Can't be too careful. Courtney here has scared off intruders a couple of times since your aunt's death."

"Intruders?" Blair turned to her in surprise.

The police chief answered for her. "Probably

just teens intent on mischief. But everybody here looks out for everybody else.'' He switched off his flashlight and hooked it onto his belt before offering a handshake. ''Welcome to Devil's Cove, Mr. Colby.''

''Thanks.'' Blair returned the handshake.

''You plan on staying, or just here to go over your aunt's things?''

''I'll be here at least for the summer.''

''I see.'' Boyd looked up at the voice squawking over the squad car's radio. ''I'd better answer that call.''

As he strolled away, Blair turned to Courtney. ''Any more questions?''

''Sorry. I thought it best to err on the side of caution.''

''You're right, of course. Thanks for keeping an eye on my aunt's place. But now, if you'll excuse me, it's been a long day.'' Deliberately turning his back on Courtney, he picked up his duffel and stepped inside, closing the door in her face.

Feeling more than a little foolish, she picked her way over the lawn and climbed the stairs to her apartment. From her balcony she could see the lights winking on in the windows of the Colby cottage. It seemed strange to think of someone being there. Strange and sad.

She'd been a fool to allow herself to begin thinking of it as hers. Once again, it would seem, all her carefully laid plans had been thwarted by a man. From the little she'd seen of him, an arrogant man, as well.

No big deal, she thought with a sigh. Story of her life.

Chapter 2

Blair stepped into the tiny kitchen of the cottage and switched on the light, pleased to find the power on. A phone call before he left Boston had restored both power and water, and for that he was grateful. The tiny refrigerator in the old-fashioned kitchen was humming.

It seemed odd to see all the cupboard doors open, packages and cans spilled over onto the counter. As though someone had been shuffling through them. The curtains were drawn tightly over the windows, as if to hold out the light. The floor, too, was littered with cans and boxes, almost obliterating the little rugs his aunt enjoyed making out of strips of colorful rags.

He closed his eyes and could hear her voice reading aloud from her beloved books. Every wall in this little cottage was lined with shelves crammed with books. She'd read to him from the classics. From fairy tales, which seemed to thrill her more than him. And, of course, her beloved mysteries, which they had both loved.

He stepped through the tiny dinette into the living room and stopped in his tracks. Every shelf had been swept clean of books. They now lay in a jumble on the floor.

Alarmed, he made his way to the bedroom, the floor just as littered with his aunt's books and knickknacks. He stood in the middle of the room, his mind reeling. Why would anyone do such a thing?

The police chief had said teen vandals had tried to break in in the past. Was that what this was?

A slow, seething fury began building inside him. This was why the curtains had been drawn across the windows. Not out of respect for the woman who had died here, but to hide the vandalism. He strode across the room and drew open the curtains, revealing the window latch that had been forced. It had been an easy matter to sneak inside, go from room to room and leave without anyone being the wiser.

He leaned a hip against the wall and studied his aunt's bedroom. Footprints crisscrossed the dust that layered the floor. Careful not to disturb anything, he picked his way back to the kitchen and fished his cell phone from his duffel. After dialing the police, he leaned wearily against the counter.

The mattress of his aunt's double bed was bare of linens, but after fifteen hours on the road, it still managed to look inviting. Not that he'd get much time to enjoy it.

He sighed. And prepared himself for a very long night.

"What a mess." Chief Boyd Thompson watched as his assistant dusted for fingerprints, though in his gut he'd already dismissed any chance of finding the vandals. "Still, it could have been worse."

"Really? How do you figure?" Too restless to sit, Blair was pacing the tiny kitchen.

"Sometimes when these kids are through, they toss a match to hide the destruction." The police chief frowned. "I'm thinking the summer crowd. Looking for some action while spending their vacation in dullsville. Doesn't look like something our regular kids would do.''

Blair shrugged. "What makes you so certain it was kids?"

"Just an educated guess." The chief pointed to the food on the counter. "A thief wouldn't stop to think about food. He'd just take what he could carry and run. I figure after they had their fun, they went looking for munchies. Soda. Or maybe hoping to find booze.''

Even while he seethed about anyone going through his aunt's belongings, Blair had to admit to himself that it made sense.

When the young police officer stepped into the kitchen, plastic bags in hand, the chief offered a handshake. "Sorry you had to endure such a lousy welcome. But I'm glad you called us right away. We'll test those shoe prints, and hope for some fingerprints, as well. If there's anything in our records with a match, we'll find them."

"Thanks, Chief.''

Blair waited until the police car was gone before walking to the bedroom.

There were clean linens in his car, but he was too weary to fetch them. Instead he opened the bedroom window and watched the fresh breeze off the lake send the stale curtains billowing like sails.

Switching off the light he stripped and settled himself on the bare mattress.

He wouldn't think about the vandalism. Wouldn't think about strangers sneaking around his aunt's cottage. All he would think about now was the fact that, for the first time in years, he felt as if he'd truly come home.

He was asleep instantly.

Courtney pulled a simple silk tank over her head before slipping into an ankle-skimming skirt the color of a ripe peach and fastening the straps of cool white sandals. As she straightened she tossed back her hair, sending it rippling down her back in a cascade of burnished chestnut. Picking up a sprinkling can, she tended to her morning ritual, watering all her plants on the balcony.

She thought she heard a knock on the door downstairs just as the coffee began to perk. Couldn't people read the sign? Surely they could wait another hour until she was open for business.

When the knock sounded again, louder, she set her cup aside and with a sigh, started down the stairs. Although most deliveries were made during business hours, there was always the chance that something had been shipped overnight and needed immediate attention.

When she yanked open the door, the uniform wasn't that of a delivery man, but rather of a successful businessman.

Courtney's reaction to Blair Colby, standing on the threshold, was even stronger than it had been the previous night. Especially now that she could see, in the clear light of morning, just how handsome and perfectly groomed this man was—two things that instantly sent off warnings in her brain. She'd learned the hard way that men with too much charm and good looks felt they didn't need to play by the rules of ordinary people.

With his crisp white shirt, carefully knotted tie and suit jacket anchored over his shoulder by a thumb, he could have been a *GQ* model. Especially with that lock of dark hair spilling over his forehead at just the perfect rakish angle. His eyes were hidden behind sunglasses.

"Good morning, Ms. Brennan."

"It's Courtney."

"Courtney." He was as unsmiling as he'd been the night before. "Sorry to bother you, but I have a cleaning crew coming over today, and I can't wait around for them. I wonder if I could leave the key to my aunt's place with you?"

She could be just as brusque as Blair Colby.

"Of course." She held out her hand. "Too busy to clean it yourself?"

"I'd intended to. But there's too much mess. Someone trashed the cottage."

"Trashed the—" She blinked. "But I've been so careful to watch for any intruders."

"Which is why whoever did it broke in on the far side, away from prying eyes. Chief Thompson said it's a good bet they came by boat after dark and left the same way."

"He was here?" She'd heard the sound of a car, but thought it was just her new neighbor, out to one of the late-night restaurants or clubs.

"Yeah. He figures it was teens bent on a night of adventure."

"I'm sorry. Was there much damage?"

"None that I could see." He slipped off his sunglasses and pinched the bridge of his nose. "They just tossed all my aunt's things around, probably helped themselves to food from the cupboards and then left feeling pretty pleased."

Courtney could see the warring of anger and frustration in his eyes. "You haven't had much of a homecoming, have you?" Despite her misgivings, her tender heart betrayed her. "Would you like some coffee?"

He sniffed the air. "I didn't know if that coffee

smell was coming from your place or if I'd died and gone to heaven.''

She wasn't going to be swayed by a little flattery, she thought. But good manners had her opening the door wider. ''I just made a fresh pot. Why don't you come upstairs?''

''I'd love to.'' He stepped inside and followed her up the stairs. ''I know my aunt had a coffeemaker somewhere in those cupboards, but I didn't have the energy to wade through the mess to find it.''

While Courtney reached for another cup, Blair glanced around the tiny space with a look of appreciation. ''If I didn't know I was in northern Michigan, I'd swear I was in a villa in Tuscany.''

She handed him a steaming cup. ''That was my intention.''

Up close, his eyes were silver gray and fixed on her with the same intensity he'd used to examine the room. It was a most unsettling feeling, as though he'd already catalogued everything about her and filed it away for future reference. She couldn't decide if he was being arrogant, or it was simply his nature to examine everybody and everything under a microscope.

While she picked up her cup he took the time to look around more carefully. The walls and ceiling had been faux painted in soft shades of umber and terra-cotta. A faded floral rug softened the hardwood floor. One corner of the room was dominated by an antique desk and an armchair in deep rich brocade. In front of the fireplace was an inviting sofa mounded with pillows in the same muted tones as the walls. There was the sound of a fountain on the little balcony, where a metal table and chairs seemed to be surrounded by colorful pots of trailing ivy and flowers.

"This is amazing. How much of it did you do yourself?"

"Most of it. I hired a handyman for the really heavy work. And a local firm handles the electrical and plumbing. My sisters give me a hand whenever I need it. But for the most part, I just do what pleases me. This was a series of small rooms until I had the walls removed."

He studied the stencil of a vine curving over the curved doorway. "Where did you study design?"

Courtney arched a brow. "How do you know I did?"

"It's obvious."

She sipped her coffee. "New York first. Then Milan and Paris."

"Really? So did I. But then I wound up in the

Greek Isles and thought I might never come home.''

''You're in interior design?''

He shook his head. ''Architecture. I've been hired to design the clubhouse for the yacht and tennis club.''

''I see.'' She led the way to the balcony. ''So that's why you came. It wasn't necessarily for the pleasure of staying in your aunt's cottage.''

''That's right. I just figured, since I was coming here anyway, I'd revisit the place I spent my childhood summers.'' He draped his jacket over the back of the chair and, instead of sitting, walked to the railing and studied the cottage from this perspective.

''Do you think your work will be finished by the end of the summer?''

He shrugged his shoulders. ''Hard to say. But if things aren't going well, I'll just stay on until the job is completed.''

''But that could be six months or more.'' She hoped he hadn't heard the note of alarm in her voice. A summer was one thing. Another year of uncertainty about whether or not she could have the cottage was asking too much.

He nodded and turned away to lean a hip against the railing. ''I believe in being a hands-on architect. If my name's on the contract, I'm going to be here until my client is satisfied with the work.'' He gave a grim smile. ''Even if it means waiting until the furniture is in place and the guests are arriving for the grand opening.''

Courtney sipped. ''If you're planning on staying that long, I don't understand why you wouldn't want something more comfortable than your aunt's cottage. I've heard that the new waterfront condos they've built for the executives are really lavish.''

''After reading the glossy brochure they sent me, I have to admit I found it tempting.''

Fresh hope surged through Courtney, and she set down her cup so quickly she could feel the hot liquid splash over the edge. ''I'm sure that old cottage must seem pretty primitive.''

He was studying her with interest. ''Not primitive, but simple. It isn't luxury I crave. I remember spending summers here with my aunt when I was a boy. I hadn't really given it much thought until your letter. And then I decided I'd like to take a sentimental summer in the old cottage before I decide whether or not to sell.''

''So you might be willing to sell to me when your work here is finished?''

''I might.'' He looked out over the water. ''I

can see why you'd want it. That's an amazing view.''

Which meant the price had just gone up, she thought with a wave of annoyance. ''You'll probably need a lot of things to make your stay comfortable.''

He kept his back to her, studying the path of a sailboat far out on Lake Michigan. ''I'll get busy making a list.'' He turned back to face her. ''If your apartment is any indication of the quality of goods in your shop, I ought to be able to find plenty of the things I need right here.''

''Feel free to look around my shop. What I don't have, the other stores in town can provide.''

He finished his coffee and started toward the stairs. ''Thanks for your hospitality. And for holding the key until the cleaning crew gets here.''

''It's no trouble.'' Courtney managed a smile as she followed him down the stairs. ''I hope your aunt's things weren't destroyed.''

''Mostly they were just tossed onto the floor. I'm sure a few of the more fragile porcelains will be broken, but the books will survive.'' He opened the door and slipped on his sunglasses before turning to her. Once again his eyes were hidden. ''I guess I'll be seeing you around.''

She watched as he climbed into a vintage red

Corvette parked at the curb. The car suited him, she decided. Smooth. Slick. The image of laid-back casual elegance that came with a satisfying career.

Why would an obviously successful architect want to spend a summer in a deserted cottage, when he could have all the amenities of a luxurious condominium?

Unless he thought, by making her wait, he could double the price.

She could feel all her plans for the future coming apart at the seams. And there wasn't a thing she could do about it.

Blair Colby might be movie-star handsome, but to Courtney that didn't mean a thing. Looks aside, she found him to be a little too smug, a bit too annoying. Like a certain someone from her past who'd taught her a lesson she wouldn't soon forget. There was a breed of man who thought that all he needed to get through life was looks and charm. She'd bought into that once. Never again.

She finished her coffee and decided to get an early start on her books. She was not in the mood to face the bills, but it would take her mind off the fact that, for the summer and possibly longer, her plans for the Colby cottage had just gone up in smoke.

Chapter 3

After a satisfying day at work, Blair turned his car onto the narrow gravel path that led to his aunt's cottage. Last night he'd been afraid to trust it. By the light of day he could see that it was just wide enough to accommodate his vehicle. Outside the door he rolled to a stop and snatched up his suit jacket before stepping out.

Once inside the cottage he looked around with a smile of pleasure. The cleaning crew he'd hired had done their job well. The rooms smelled of disinfectant. Late-afternoon sunshine spilled through gleaming windows. His aunt's curtains had been returned to their spotless condition.

He opened the refrigerator and noted with satisfaction that the groceries he'd ordered had been delivered and put away, as he'd requested.

Despite the cleaning odors, he could almost smell his aunt Sarah's biscuits. She'd called them tea biscuits, and had always served them with a little pot of homemade strawberry preserves.

In the bedroom he stripped and carefully hung his clothes before slipping into swim trunks. After so many summers of Sarah's stern reprimands, it was second nature to pick up after himself. His aunt had set great store by neatness.

He gave a last glance at the bed, made up with fresh linens, before dashing out the door and racing toward the water.

He'd spent the day walking the entire complex with the contractors and the board of directors. He'd gone over the blueprints with them, answered their questions about time frames for the various stages of development for this multimillion-dollar project, and had smoothly discussed local and state ordinances that would have to be met. He'd listened to their complaints, their fears, their labor troubles. By the end of the day he'd assured them that their baby would be delivered on time, within budget and without any unhealthy side effects. All part of the job.

He raced to the end of the rickety dock and took a neat dive into the water. It was as frigid as he'd always remembered. After the first numbing shock that left him breathless, he surfaced, shook water from his hair, and with powerful strokes, swam into the deep until his lungs were straining.

Turning onto his back, he stared up at the cool blue sky and grinned like a kid on Christmas morning. His workday had just ended. Now, he thought, it was playtime for Blair.

He had Courtney Brennan to thank for this mindless, childhood pleasure. He'd pretty much put aside all thought of Devil's Cove in the years he'd spent abroad. Until he'd landed this job, there'd been no time to think about the town where he'd spent his summers. Even after accepting this offer, he'd been considering a move into one of the new condos while he completed his contract.

And then that letter had arrived asking to purchase his aunt's cottage. It had piqued his interest, and he realized that he needed to see it once more.

He smiled again as he started back to shore. It had all come together so perfectly. The opportunity to work on this project. And a chance to spend one last summer in the only place he'd ever felt completely at home.

Odd that he should think that. He'd first come here as a frightened eight-year-old, still reeling from spending six months with his father and new stepmother, and six months with his mother and new stepfather. He'd never been close to his aunt Sarah, a spinster, who considered a child, even one related to her, to be an intrusion into her carefully structured lifestyle. She had greeted him not with hugs but with a handshake. Instead of sympathy, she gave him chores. Although there were no lectures, she made it abundantly clear that there were rules that could not be broken for any reason. And always, late into the night, instead of goodnight kisses, she read from her store of precious books.

Back then he'd arrived in Devil's Cove with a feeling of dread. Over the course of the summer he'd discovered simple pleasures. Fresh fruit, warmed by the sun and eaten freshly picked from the orchards that abounded in the area. A plunge into the icy waters of Lake Michigan after the hot, dirty gardening had been tended to, and the chores completed to Sarah's liking. And best of all books, into which a lonely, confused little boy could escape the harsh realities of his life. As the years hurried by, from prep school to college, and his parents continued their dance of changing partners, he returned each summer to the only constant in his life. This cottage had become his refuge, and his aunt, however reluctant, had become his anchor.

Blair pulled himself up onto the end of the dock and picked up the towel he'd dropped. Draping it around his hips he strode to the cottage and began firing up the little grill he'd bought in town. By the time his steak was sizzling over the coals, he'd pulled on shorts and a tee and was seated at a wooden picnic table, sipping a cold beer.

As he walked to the grill to turn the steak he glanced up to see a little sailboat dancing across the waves, and made a mental note to look into buying one for himself. In his youth, the only boat his aunt would permit was an ancient wooden skiff so heavy it took the two of them, rowing furiously, just to go around the bend.

The thought had him smiling. To Aunt Sarah, even the task of rowing became a lesson to be learned. She would pass the time regaling him with the history of Devil's Cove and the lore of pirates and treasure, bound to stir the imagination of a lonely boy.

He picked up his beer and realized that the little sailboat was heading directly toward his dock. While he watched, the sail was lowered, the anchor dropped and the lone figure aboard cut cleanly into the water and started swimming.

Courtney braced for the cold water, seconds before she went under. When she surfaced, she started swimming toward the cottage with smooth, strong strokes.

It wasn't until she reached the shallows and stepped onto the shore that she realized she wasn't alone. From the deck of the boat, the only thing she'd seen was the cottage. Now that she realized Blair Colby was standing there watching her, there was nothing to do but acknowledge him and move on.

"Sorry." She paused on the banks. "I didn't mean to intrude on your dinner."

"You're not." He couldn't help staring at the water sheeting down her legs. Such long, tanned legs. They'd been hidden earlier this morning under that ankle-length skirt. "I'll get you a towel."

"Don't bother. I can get one at my place."

He ignored her protest and walked inside, returning moments later with an oversize beach towel.

"Thanks." Courtney wrapped it around herself like a sarong, tucking the ends into the top of her bikini and turned, determined to make an escape.

"Want a beer?"

"No, thanks."

"Look." He laid a hand on her arm. Her skin was cool from the lake and still damp. But the heat that shot from his fingertips all the way up his arm had him drawing away quickly. "I know I came on a bit strong last night and again this morning. But I'd really like to thank you."

"For what?" The look she gave him was equally cool.

"If it weren't for your letter, I wouldn't be here."

At his admission she arched a brow in surprise.

Using the distraction to his advantage, he unscrewed the top of a frosty bottle of beer and handed it to her before picking up his own. "I'd originally planned on staying in the new executive condos down by the waterfront while I put in my time on this project. After the firm forwarded your letter to me, I decided I wanted another summer in my aunt's cottage before I gave it up."

She took a long sip. "So you do intend to sell it?"

He shrugged. "I won't make any promises, except one. If I decide to sell, you'll get the first shot at buying."

She managed a dry laugh. "Thanks, I think. I'll

let you know how grateful I am after I hear the price you set.''

He grinned and nodded toward the boat bobbing offshore. ''I was admiring your boat before I knew it was yours.''

''Are you a sailor?''

''I like to think so.''

''Then I'll make you a deal. If you allow me to anchor it here, you can take it out whenever I'm not using it.''

''That's generous of you. What if I wreck it?''

She gave him a level look. ''Then you'll owe me a new one.''

''Ouch. Guess I'd better brush up on my sailing skills before I take you up on that. Where have you been anchoring it?''

''At my sister's place a mile or so from here. I sail on the lake most evenings, if the weather permits. Anytime you'd like to join me, just say so.''

''I'll do that.'' He lifted the steak from the fire. ''There's more than enough if you'd like to share.''

Courtney was already shaking her head. ''I'll leave you to it. I have a seafood salad chilling in my apartment.''

''Why don't you bring it down? We'll share.''

She seemed to be considering it when he added,

"I picked up a strawberry cheesecake at The Pier on my way home."

"Strawberry cheesecake." She sighed. "That's one of my weaknesses. And The Pier makes the best around. How can I resist? Be right back." She set aside her beer and danced lightly across the yard. A short time later she returned wearing a terry beach robe and carrying a covered dish.

Blair had added another place setting to the picnic table and was dividing the steak.

She lifted the lid of the bowl to reveal chunks of shrimp, crab and lobster on a bed of greens.

As she spooned some onto Blair's plate, he picked up a piece of crabmeat and tasted. "No doubt about it. I'm getting the better end of this deal."

"Oh, I don't know about that." Courtney cut a small piece off her steak and nibbled. "There's not much that can beat a steak cooked on the grill. And then there's dessert."

"Got a sweet tooth, do you?"

She merely smiled while she watched him tuck into his meal. Then she did the same.

"Sailing always leaves me hungry. That's why I made sure I had something ready to eat as soon as I got home." She laughed. "Of course, I didn't realize I'd be eating all this."

"Where was home before Devil's Cove?"

"This is where I grew up. I lived here until college."

He picked up his beer. "And then?"

"Italy. Rome first, then Milan."

He saw the little frown that furrowed her brow at the mention of that city. "How long have you been back?"

"A year, give or take a few months."

"Planning on staying?"

She nodded. "At least for now. I wasn't sure at first, but I've discovered a lot of things about this place that I'd forgotten."

He sat back. "I know what you mean. Today, while I was driving through the town, so many things came back to me. Getting up before dawn to dig for night crawlers before going fishing. Working up a sweat riding my bike to town for ice cream after supper. Lying on that little porch of my aunt's, staring up at the stars and wondering where I'd be when I grew up, and what I'd be doing." He stared at the water. "I found myself looking at the blueprints for the club and marina in a whole new way, and thinking what fun it would be to have a cruiser on Lake Michigan."

"Fun and expensive," she said with a laugh.

"Maybe. But certainly worth the price just to skim the waves and feel the surge of power."

Courtney shrugged. "Too noisy. I've always craved the silence of a sailboat and the thrill of the wind filling the sails. I can still skim the waves, but the only sound I hear is the flap of the canvas and the birds wheeling overhead. There's a sense of peace out there that's like nothing else."

He laughed. "All right. You've sold me. Maybe next time you go sailing, I'll go along." He pushed away from the table and went into the cottage. Minutes later he returned with a tray laden with coffee and mugs, and two slices of cheesecake drizzled with strawberry preserves and garnished with fresh strawberries.

Courtney nodded toward the cottage. "Is it as you remembered it?"

He nodded as he handed her a steaming mug of coffee. "Pretty much. A lot smaller, though."

"Maybe that's because you've grown bigger since you were last here." She accepted a plate and tucked into her dessert. "How long ago was that?"

"Too many years." He shrugged. "I was here a time or two during college, but not since. There was no time during my postgrad days. And then I was off to see the world.''

Courtney studied him over the rim of her cup. ''Funny how the world can seem so glamorous, until you've had a chance to see it up close. A year ago I'd have said that no amount of money would entice me to come back to Devil's Cove. But here I am, not only home, but loving it.''

He frowned as he polished off the last bite of cheesecake. ''I almost refused this offer, because I thought I'd be bored out of my mind in this town after twenty-four hours.''

Courtney arched a brow. ''Bored yet?''

He gave her a measured look that brought a rush of heat to her cheeks. ''Not yet. How about you?''

''No time.'' She pushed away from the table and began gathering up her dishes, which she placed on the empty tray. ''Thanks for sharing your dinner. And the cheesecake was divine.''

''So was the company.''

His words, spoken directly behind her, had her pausing. When she turned, he was so close, their bodies were nearly touching. That same probing look was in his eyes, sending a prickly sensation skittering along her spine.

He touched a hand to her arm, and she stepped

back a pace, until she felt the scrape of the picnic table against her hips.

"Sorry if I startled you." He held up the covered salad bowl, now empty. "I didn't want you to forget this."

"Thank you." She accepted it from his hand and waited for him to move aside.

Instead, he stepped closer. "I don't bite, Courtney."

She lifted her chin. "I should hope not. Now if you'll excuse me…"

He took her hand in his, and she flinched as he lifted it, his eyes steady on hers. "Do you have something against me, or do you dislike being touched by any man?"

"I don't dislike…" She saw the quick flash of humor in his eyes and gave a huff of disgust. "I take that back. I do resent being touched by you. Now if you'll step aside…"

"So, it's personal."

"Yes. No." She tried to pull her hand free, but he tightened his grasp. That only fueled her anger. "Call it a survival instinct. Unless you get out of my way, I'm going to haul off and let you have it with this salad bowl."

He surprised her by roaring with laughter. "What a terrible waste of a pretty dish. But since you insist…'' He lifted her hand to his mouth and brushed a kiss over the palm before closing her hand around the kiss.

She knew her eyes were wide with shock, but she was too stunned to compose herself.

That had his smile widening. He lowered his mouth to hers and brushed a soft kiss over her lips.

At her quick intake of breath he chuckled before whispering, ''Trust me. That was personal.''

''So is this.'' With a look that would have wilted a stronger man she gave him a shove before turning away and fleeing to the safety of her apartment.

Chapter 4

"Oh, look, Jenny." A pretty tourist, wearing shorts and a tank top that showed off her tan to its best advantage, pointed to a framed print hanging on the gallery wall of Treasures. "I love this artist's work."

Her friend, whose blond ponytail streamed out the back of a bright green baseball cap, nodded. "Sidney Brennan. I think I read somewhere that she lives right here in Devil's Cove."

"Really?" Curious, the tourist stepped closer to study the painting of a pair of Canada geese standing guard over their young on the banks of a river. "I bet Dan would love this for his office."

Courtney crossed the room. "Would you like me to move it to the window, so you can get a better view?"

"Oh, would you?"

While Courtney held it up, the two women stood together, watching the play of fading sunlight on the canvas.

Courtney invited them to step closer. "You'd swear you could almost touch the feathers."

"It's true." The tourist sighed. "I wasn't planning on spending this much, but I have to have this for my husband."

Courtney dimpled. "He's going to love you for it. Would you like me to wrap it for shipping, or do you want to take it with you?"

"I'll have it sent." She looked at the mound of merchandise she'd already stacked on the counter, alongside the things her friend had purchased. "It's one less thing I won't have to deal with when our vacation is over."

"How much longer will you be in Devil's Cove?" Courtney handed the woman a shipping form.

"We leave at the end of the week." The woman sighed as she filled in her name and address. "I wish we could spend the entire summer here."

Her words had Courtney smiling. "I take it you've been having a good time."

"The best." She waited while Courtney tabulated her other purchases before handing over her credit card. "And finding this Sidney Brennan print is the frosting on the cake. My friend thinks she lives around here."

Courtney nodded. "She does." She handed the woman a receipt. "One of our hometown success stories."

"What I wouldn't give to meet her."

"Oh, she's pretty ordinary." Seeing the woman's look of shock, Courtney added with a laugh, "Sorry. I couldn't resist teasing you a bit. Actually, she's shy and sweet and something of a loner. I ought to know. Sidney is my sister."

"You're kidding." The young woman slowly nodded. "Now I understand why you have such an amazing selection of her paintings. I found one or two in several other shops in town, but nothing like this."

"It does give me an unfair advantage over the other merchants." Courtney picked up the shipping form. "This will probably arrive at your home just about the time you do."

"Thank you. I just love your shop. And be sure you tell your sister how much I love her work."

"I will. Come back again."

The two women left, juggling several shopping bags.

Courtney saw Kendra out back, gesturing to the lovely stone benches while a white-haired man nodded and smiled. Today Kendra was wearing a pair of faded bell-bottoms and a baggy top that looked as though it had been woven of string. On anyone else it would have looked ridiculous, especially with that orange spiky hair. But Kendra managed to pull it off.

Minutes later the white-haired man was following Kendra inside where she rang up a sale.

"I assume you'll want this shipped?" Kendra asked.

"No, ma'am. Got my truck parked just around the corner. I'll be right over to pick it up."

When he left, Kendra and Courtney exchanged knowing smiles.

"He's been sitting there for over an hour," Kendra explained. "I was pretty sure he was going to buy it."

"Good instincts."

The girl chuckled. "I told you. Someday I'm going to own my own place. Not exactly like this. Too predictable," she muttered. "But more like, you know, loaded with people's cast-offs and stuff.''

"Like a thrift shop?"

"Sort of." She stared out the window until a brand-new bright red truck pulled up to the curb and her customer and a younger man stepped out. Under Kendra's direction, they loaded the stone bench into the back of the pickup and drove away.

Inside, Kendra picked up her denim purse and waved to her boyfriend, leaning against a lamp-post outside the door. "See you in the morning, Courtney."

"Yeah. Thanks." Courtney followed her to the door and flipped over the sign before locking up for the evening. She'd been tempted to close up more than an hour earlier, but she'd sensed that these last stragglers were serious shoppers. She was glad now that she'd followed her instincts. That extra hour would just about pay this month's overhead.

Upstairs in her apartment she slipped out of her clothes and into a white bikini. Tucking a cover-up and sandals into her sea bag, she stepped lightly down the stairs and across the yard. As she passed the Colby cottage, she noted with relief that Blair's car wasn't in the driveway.

She'd missed a good deal of sleep last night

over Blair Colby. Not that she would ever let him know that. She'd already decided that the next time she saw him she would be so cool he would wonder if he'd only imagined that kiss.

Now if only she could fool herself into believing the same thing. It was, after all, nothing more than a kiss. But the heat from it had lingered far into the night, leaving her tossing and turning like a lovestruck teen.

No matter. She wasn't falling into that trap again.

Clipping the strap of her waterproof bag around her waist she stepped into the water and began swimming toward her sailboat. Once there she tossed the bag into the boat, before pulling herself over the rail. Within minutes she was manning the sails as the little craft left the cove behind and followed the rounded shoreline toward the big houses in the distance.

''Blair.'' Charlotte Brennan opened the front door of The Willows to greet the handsome young man standing there. ''Did you have any trouble finding it?''

''None at all, Charley. Your directions were easy enough.''

''Come in.'' She stood aside and watched his

reaction as he stared around the elegant foyer of the home.

He turned to her with a smile. "This is spectacular."

"I knew you'd like it. That was my reaction the first time I saw it as a young bride."

"You live here now?"

She nodded before leading the way along the hallway with its colorful Spanish tiles. "My in-laws added a wing of the house for us, and Christopher and I lived here with them while raising our four daughters." She laughed lightly. "I know that wouldn't work for most people, but it suited us perfectly. In fact, even now that Christopher has passed away, I've never given a thought to leaving."

"I don't blame you." They stepped into the kitchen, where a woman was just removing something from the oven. The wonderful fragrance of freshly-baked bread had him salivating, even as the sight of the cook had him grinning. She was as round as she was tall, and her short white hair was the consistency of cotton balls.

"Trudy, this is the young architect I was telling you about. Blair Colby, this is Trudy Carpenter. Trudy's been with the Brennan family since they first moved here, more than fifty years ago."

"There you go, Charley." After a lifetime of smoking, the old woman's gravelly voice was as deep as a man's. "Giving away my age again." She looked Blair over carefully. "You Sarah Colby's kin?"

"Nephew."

"Tough old bird."

Blair laughed. "That she was."

"I liked her."

"That makes two of us."

Trudy's look softened. She turned to Charley. "The others are out on the patio. As usual the judge is busy ruining the beef tenderloin on the grill. And using one of his latest inventions to do the job. You might want to remind him that some meats don't need to be charred to be digestible."

Charley sighed. "I'll do my best, Trudy." She turned toward the French doors. "Come on, Blair. It's time you met the rest of my family." She led the way, with Blair trailing behind her.

As they stepped out onto the brick-paved patio, Blair paused a moment to take it all in. Ivy softened the brick-and-stone walls of the elegant old mansion. Like the interior, the patio, with its charming urns of flowers and vines, and lovely mix of antique iron furniture and contemporary glass table and cushioned chairs, was an architect's dream. Added to that was a broad expanse of manicured lawn that ran clear to the water's edge. Against the blue sky and the deeper blue-green of Lake Michigan, white sails of boats in the distance made it a postcard-perfect scene.

For a moment Blair wondered at the number of people milling about. Could this all be one family?

His hostess handled the introductions. "Blair Colby, my in-laws. Judge Frank Brennan and his wife, Bert."

"Sir. Mrs. Brennan." He offered his handshake.

Charley turned to a tiny, flame-haired young woman who was smiling shyly. "This is my daughter Sidney."

"The artist who'll be doing the mural at the entrance to the clubhouse." He offered his hand. "I admire your work."

"Thank you. It's nice to meet you, Blair."

Charley included a leggy blonde holding a little boy in her arms and the man beside her holding the hand of a boy of about four. "My daughter Hannah and her husband, Ethan Harrison, and sons Danny and T.J."

Blair shook the man's hand and high-fived the boys before turning to Hannah. "I was just looking over your design sketches for the landscaping.'' He grinned at the judge. ''You've got quite a talented family, sir.''

''Indeed we do.'' Frank winked at his wife, who merely smiled fondly around the circle.

''Blair, this is my daughter Emily and her husband, Jason Cooper.''

''Everyone in town talks about you, Dr. Brennan. It's nice to meet you, Emily.'' He turned to Jason. ''I'd heard that you'd left Malibu and were writing in Devil's Cove now. I suppose, with its background of pirates and rumrunners, it would make a great setting for a few thrillers.''

Jason chuckled. ''I'm keeping it in mind in case I ever run out of ideas.''

''As if that would ever happen,'' his wife said with a laugh.

Trudy stepped out with a tray of drinks, and Blair joined the men in helping himself to a frosty mug of beer.

Frank Brennan returned to the grill, with his daughter-in-law beside him to lend a hand. Blair found himself fascinated with the odd implement in the older man's hand. It looked to be part fork, part spatula and demanded a great deal of attention as he flipped the meat, turned it, twisted it and, in general, seemed to be trying to torture it.

In an aside Trudy whispered, "The judge fancies himself an inventor. Lucky me. I get stuck with all his brilliant inventions, until I find a way to toss them without his knowledge."

Blair covered his laughter behind his hand.

Seeing the trim little sailboat skimming close to shore, Frank Brennan pointed with his invention. "Looks like the last of our band of angels is about to arrive."

Blair found himself mesmerized by the figure in the white bikini poised to dive. By the time she'd stepped from the surf and squeezed the water from her hair, he'd managed to get his heart rate back to normal. Or as normal as it would ever be when looking at Courtney Brennan.

She unzipped a bag and pulled out a length of fabric the color of strawberries. After stepping into it, she was modestly covered from neck to ankle by a long gauzy gown that seemed to cling to every curve of her damp body. Slipping her feet into matching sandals, she started toward the cluster of people on the patio.

She was smiling as she walked toward them. Blair stood in their midst, watching the sway of her hips, and was grateful for the cold mug in his hand. Instead of pressing it to his forehead as he would have liked, he merely sipped. He was still sipping his beer when she caught sight of him. Though her smile slipped a notch, to her credit she managed not to frown, though he was certain, by the fire in her eyes, she was cursing him under her breath.

It was obvious that she hadn't known he would be here.

"Well, here's our Courtney now." Frank Brennan stepped forward to kiss his granddaughter's cheek before saying, "Your mother invited a young friend to join us for dinner tonight. Courtney, may I present Blair Colby."

"We've met." She gave him a cool smile before turning to greet the rest of her family with hugs and kisses.

"You've been in Court's shop?" Hannah asked.

"Not yet. Though I'm hoping to get there soon."

"Then where did you two meet?" Emily sounded a bit too interested, causing Courtney to arch a brow. Leave it to her family to play matchmaker. To their way of thinking, anyone unmarried was fair game.

"I'm staying in my aunt's old cottage."

"The one behind Court's shop? But I thought…" Hannah put a hand over her mouth.

Blair chuckled. "Don't worry. You're not giving away any secrets. I'm aware that your sister
is interested in buying the place. I've already told
her that if I decide to sell when this project is
completed, she'll be the first one to know."

"That's great." Hannah kept an eye on the two
boys, who were now chasing butterflies across the
lawn. "I've already drawn up some ideas for the
gardens Courtney is hoping to add."

"Gardens?" He shot a glance at Courtney, who
was busy helping herself to a glass of wine from
the tray.

"Court didn't tell you?" Missing the warning
look from her sister, Hannah launched into details
about her favorite subject. "She sells these fabu-
lous stone benches that are made by a colorful old
gentleman who lives in the middle of the forest.
When Court first found him, he was barely eking
out a living. Now he's had to hire two college
students to help him keep up with the demand.
Court figures she can sell even more if she can
present them in the proper setting. So I've drawn
up a perennial patch that will resemble an English
garden with foxgloves, periwinkle and lavender,
softened with ivy and grasses, and decorated with
garden art, and of course, the old man's benches."

"Where are you planning on putting this garden?"

"In the open space between her shop and your cottage. Then, of course, there's the cutting garden, which I'm thinking would do best on that stretch of land closest to the shore. Wait until you see what I've planned around the sides of your cottage."

"Now aren't you sorry you ever got her talking about landscaping?" Hannah's husband, Ethan, drew her close and brushed a kiss over her cheek. "That's one thing she never grows tired of talking about." He linked his fingers with hers and drew her away. "Right now I think we'd better haul the boys out of your grandfather's gardens, or you're going to have some major repairs to make in the morning."

As they walked away, Blair stepped closer to Courtney. "You don't let any grass grow under your feet, do you? Gardens? Before you even knew if you could buy the place?"

She shrugged. "Hannah's got a big mouth."

He chuckled. "Sorry I spoiled your plans."

She sipped her wine. "They aren't spoiled. Just delayed."

"You're awfully sure of yourself."

"You did say you'd give me first chance to make an offer."

Blair couldn't resist bursting her bubble. "*If* I decide to sell." He cast an admiring glance around. "Now that I've seen The Willows, I just might decide to stay and turn my aunt's cottage into my dream home."

Before Courtney could make a response, her mother stepped between them to link an arm through each of theirs.

"Dinner's ready." In a whisper she added, "Thanks to my vigilance, your grandfather wasn't able to burn the tenderloin. I can't say the same about his fingers, however. His latest invention needs a bit of work." Aloud she added, "Since you two already know each other, I'd like you to sit side by side right here."

Trapped, Courtney thought. By her own mother.

Chapter 5

"You might just get the hang of grilling yet, Judge." Trudy sliced the tenderloin on a huge platter and began passing it around, along with a fresh garden salad and new potatoes. "I don't believe you burned a single thing."

"I had help." He winked at his daughter-in-law. "Charley said you'd have my hide if I ruined this pricey beef."

Blair held the platter while Courtney filled her plate. She was uncomfortably aware of him watching her with that intensity that she found so unsettling. Then it was her turn to take it from his hands and wait while he helped himself. When he looked up he caught her staring. She knew her face was flushed as she turned away and handed the platter to her brother-in-law Jason.

Blair took a bite and murmured his approval. "You can cook for me any time, Judge Brennan."

"You see?" Frank nudged Trudy as she walked past. "At least someone here appreciates my talent."

"Guests have to be polite." After topping off their glasses, Trudy set the bottle of white wine in a crystal ice bucket. "The rest of us can be as honest as we please."

The others merely chuckled at the long-standing teasing that had been going on between the judge and his housekeeper for as long as anyone could recall.

"You're an inventor, too, Judge Brennan?" As Blair picked up his knife, his shoulder brushed Courtney's, and she felt a quick slide of heat.

"That's right. Just a few simple items that help Trudy around the kitchen."

The housekeeper huffed out a breath.

When Blair's shoulder brushed Courtney's a second time, she glanced at her sister across the table, determined to ignore him. "Before I forget, Sidney, one of my customers wanted you to know that she just loves your art. A good thing, too, since she spent a fortune for your print of the geese with their young.''

"Proud Parents." Sidney's smile bloomed. ''I love that one. It's always nice to know someone else appreciates it enough to pay good money for it.''

''Ever since I've added that gallery of your work to my shop, business has increased by about fifty percent. And though I'd hate to lose all that income, I still think you ought to open your own gallery. You'd make a fortune.''

Sidney shook her head. ''I just don't have the head for business that you do, Court. I'd much rather concentrate on my art than have to worry about finding a building, paying the overhead and then having to deal with real, live customers.''

''Which explains,'' Emily said dryly, ''why you choose to live all alone in the middle of nowhere.''

''It's not that I don't like people.'' Emily's cheeks went red. ''But I just find that I work better without all those distractions around to disturb my concentration. Besides, since I paint mostly wildlife, it seems only natural that I live among them.''

''You don't need to explain,'' Bert said gently.

"We understand completely." Though they all worried about Sidney, who had become something of a recluse after a painful episode during her college days, they understood her need for solitude. "Now, if Courtney ever decides to move to a little place in the woods, we'll really worry."

That had everyone around the table laughing.

"You never know," Courtney said in defense. "Maybe I'll decide one of these days that I need to get away from people."

"Don't count on it." Frank leaned over to pat her hand. "Honey, you need people around you the same way Hannah needs her flowers."

"You know me so well, Poppie."

"Well enough to know you need at least a dozen projects going at one time to be happy."

"Speaking of a dozen different projects..." Charley looked at Blair. "I had a chance to look over the additions you've suggested for the clubhouse, and I don't know how you can come up with so many clever ideas."

Blair seemed uneasy to find himself the center of attention. He'd been enjoying the easy banter among the family members. "Thanks, Charley, but that's my job."

"Your job would have been a lot simpler without these additions."

"What did you think of them?"

She sighed. "They're gorgeous. Especially the atrium."

At that, Hannah swiveled her head to study him. "An atrium?"

He nodded. "In fact, the board of directors has already approved the name. The Conservatory. I saw your drawings for the gardens and decided that it would be a shame to lose all those plants during the winter months. This way, even in the dead of winter, with mountains of snow outside, our members can enjoy the beauty of your gardens."

"Oh, Blair. I'm..." Hannah opened her mouth, then closed it, which had everyone laughing aloud.

"Is Hannah really speechless?" Emily touched her sister's wrist, as though searching for a pulse. "She seems okay. But I have to say this is a first. Hannah, honey, are you in there? Or is this woman an imposter?"

While the others roared, Hannah gave a quick shake of her head. "An atrium. A conservatory. Whatever you call it, I love it. I can't wait to see your design."

Blair's food was forgotten, an indication that he was easily caught up in the love of his work. "It's pretty basic. The board had already approved a circular dining room, mostly glass, looking out over water on one side, golf course on the other. With the addition of little islands of live plants, it would feel much like this. Dining on your grandparents' patio all year long."

Bert seemed delighted. "What a grand idea."

Charley touched a napkin to her mouth. "Wait until you see it, Bert. You're going to love going there for dinner, especially in the winter."

Trudy wheeled out a cart loaded with a silver coffee service and a freshly baked chocolate torte, which she began to slice and pass around. Blair noticed that she saved the biggest pieces for the two little boys, Danny and T.J., whose eyes went wide with pleasure.

"Oh, I can just see it." Hannah began describing the plants and flowers she could use. "Blue and purple and white hydrangeas. Tulip vine and clematis climbing up and around an arbor. Victorian roses." She turned to Courtney. "And some of those lovely stone benches. And Sidney's watercolors on the walls. And…"

Blair sat back, enjoying the give and take among the sisters. "I can see that this has become quite the family project."

"You don't mind?" Charley glanced at him across the table.

He shook his head. "Not at all. In fact, this kind of enthusiasm is contagious. I don't think I've felt this much excitement over a project in years."

"The Brennan family has a way of doing that to you." Ethan dropped an arm around Hannah's shoulders and pressed a kiss to the tip of her nose. "When I first met Hannah, the thing I most loved about her was the joy she took in her work each day."

She gave him an impish grin. "And here I thought it was my great legs."

"Those, too." He caught her hand and lifted it to his lips, while the others joined in the laughter.

Blair found himself laughing along with them. This was, he realized, the most fun he'd had in a long time, while doing nothing more than enjoying a simple meal with interesting people.

While he sipped his coffee he watched the interaction between Courtney and her sisters. No competition here. Just a deep and abiding affection between them that was the real thing.

"Look." Danny pointed, and the entire party watched as several fireflies flitted across the yard.

Enchanted, Hannah reached for an empty goblet. "Come on. I'll show you what we used to do when we were little."

Leading the way, she and the boys dashed across the yard, letting out excited shrieks each time another dancing light was spotted.

They were soon joined in the hunt by Sidney, Emily and Courtney, each carrying a glass. It took them the better part of an hour before they'd managed to catch their prey, but at last they returned with their glasses sparkling like tiny stars.

"Can we keep them?" Danny asked.

"That wouldn't be fair," Hannah explained. "After they've entertained us, they need to be set free so they can fly home."

"'Cause they have little fireflies waiting for them?" Danny asked innocently.

"That's right." She and her sisters set the upside-down glasses and jars on the table and watched the light show. Finally, when they'd seen enough, they turned their captives loose.

Everyone fell silent as the tiny lights sailed across the lawn, winking in the darkness before disappearing. Shortly after that the two boys climbed up on their dad's lap, rubbing their eyes.

"I think we've had enough fun for one night," Ethan said with a wink. "Like our fireflies, we need to head home."

Just then the rumble of thunder had everyone looking up. As they watched, lightning snaked across the darkened sky.

Frank Brennan turned to his granddaughter and saw the way she was looking at her boat, anchored offshore. "I hope you're not thinking about trying to beat this storm home."

She shrugged. "I guess the thought crossed my mind. But I'm not that foolish."

"Good. I'm sure someone here can drive you home."

Blair reached into his pocket for his car keys. "Since we're practically living at the same address, it won't be any problem to see your granddaughter home, sir."

Frank beamed his approval. "Good. Good. That will give us an excuse to have you and Courtney here for one of our famous Sunday brunches tomorrow, before she picks up her boat."

"But, Poppie…" Before Courtney could think of a polite way to get out of it, her grandmother was already making plans.

"Oh, Frank, that's perfect. You will come with Courtney, won't you, Blair?"

He was about to refuse when he caught sight of the little pout that pursed Courtney's lips. Oh, the thought of annoying her was just too tempting.

His smile was radiant. "I'd love to. As long as you're sure I won't wear out my welcome."

"Not at all." Bert's smile included her granddaughter. "We're delighted to have both of you." She turned to the others. "Can we expect all of you for brunch?"

With murmured promises all around, the others began making their way around the circle of family with hugs and kisses before heading to their cars.

After bidding her family good-night, Courtney retrieved her sea bag and followed Blair to his car.

He held the door and waited until she was settled inside before closing it and walking around to the driver's side. As he turned the key in the ignition he was grinning like a kid.

It occurred to him that if looks were daggers, Courtney would be standing over his dead body by now. That had him chuckling aloud as he pushed the button to close the convertible top. As he secured it, he turned to her with a grin. "Wouldn't want you to get caught in the rain."

Even as he spoke, the first drops began falling on the windshield.

Courtney glanced over as he flicked on the wipers. "Is your timing always so perfect?"

"I like to think so." He put the car in gear and

they rolled along the curving ribbon of driveway, then turned onto the street, now slick with rain.

He drove slowly, avoiding the Saturday crowds that still clogged the heart of town. Many were just exiting shops and restaurants, some making mad dashes through the rain while others snapped open umbrellas and strolled at a more leisurely pace.

"When I spent my summers here, I used to love the rain."

Courtney couldn't hide her surprise. "So did I. But I figured I was the only one. Why did you love it?"

Blair shrugged. "It's hard to explain. I knew I couldn't go swimming or boating, or do any of the things most kids loved to do during the summer in Devil's Cove. But it always seemed like a special day to me, because my aunt Sarah used rainy days to write in a journal she kept, leaving me to my own devices. Except for a few household chores, I was free to explore."

"Where did you go?"

"Everywhere. I used to hike up to Devil's Leap."

"But that's miles from town."

He laughed. "What are a few miles to a kid with a wild imagination and an entire day to call his own?'' He thought a minute. ''And I used to crawl through all the caves around the old light-house.''

''Alone?'' The very thought had Courtney shivering.

''I never had anyone willing to go with me. So I'd take my trusty flashlight along and search for treasure.''

''Did you ever find any?''

He nodded. ''I found a rusty knife, some wood shards that I was convinced belonged to a pirate's chest, and a couple of gold coins.''

''Did you have them appraised?''

He shook his head. ''I kept them in an old box that held a bunch of my treasures. But they got lost in one of my many moves, and I never saw them again.''

''Your family moved a lot?''

''Yeah.'' He shrugged and quickly changed the subject. ''How about you? What'd you do on rainy days?''

''Bert and Trudy always had adventures planned. They were always something special. Sometimes we'd walk through town in the rain and explore all the shops. Sometimes Poppie would take us for long drives up into the hills. But my favorite was when Bert and Trudy would allow each of us to do something that appealed just to us. When it was Sidney's turn, we knew we'd all end up painting. With Hannah, it was always some sort of gardening. Emily was into doctoring strays. The more the merrier. But when it was my turn to choose, I'd always ask if I could decorate one of the rooms. I'd haul out old vases and lamps from the attic, and wonderful old portraits of ancestors that had been stored up there. Sometimes I'd fill a crystal vase with seashells I'd collected, and Poppie would allow me to cut fresh flowers from his garden. And then we'd get all dressed up and sit in my room.''

"I can see you come by your decorating skills naturally.'' He chuckled. "But I bet your sisters weren't too happy with your choices.''

She joined in the laughter. "I never thought much about it. But you're right. They could never work up much enthusiasm for hauling stuff out of the attic.''

"Can you blame them? Of course, now those things would fetch a pretty price in your shop.''

She nodded. "So would those gold coins of yours. I wonder what ever happened to them?''

He turned into their shared driveway. "We'll never know.'' He switched off the ignition and walked around to open her door, offering a hand as he did.

She ignored his hand and stepped out.

"Still being defensive, I see."

At that she went very still. "Sorry. It's hard to break old habits. I don't mean to be rude." Raindrops kissed her cheeks as she lifted her face. "Thanks for the ride. I wasn't too happy about leaving my boat anchored overnight. But I have to admit this was much better than sailing through a storm."

She saw the way his smile faded as he stared down into her eyes.

His voice was rough. "I don't think we avoided it."

"What?"

"The storm."

He lowered his head, and his mouth covered hers in a kiss that put the thunder and lightning to shame. Heat rushed through her, leaving her trembling, until she was forced to wrap her arms around his waist or risk falling.

The kiss seemed to spin on and on until it had her breath backing up in her throat. And still his mouth moved over hers, creating the most amazing fireworks behind her closed eyes.

He hadn't planned any of this. It had simply

happened, with no rhyme or reason. But now that he was holding her, kissing her, he couldn't seem to stop. She had the most incredible lips. Made for kissing. And the taste of her, cool as raindrops, sweet as summer flowers, had him hungry for more. Ever since that first kiss at his cottage, he'd known he had to taste her again.

He ran his hands lightly down her back and felt her trembling response. Despite the modest cover-up, he was all too aware of that sexy white bikini, revealing every line and curve of her body. The thought of it made him sweat.

The sound of her little moan had him lifting his head. His eyes narrowed on her, loving the way she looked in the rain. Hair wet and curling, skin glistening with raindrops, the gown now clinging to her like a second skin.

"You'd better get inside."

She nodded, afraid to trust her voice.

As she turned away he called, "I forgot to ask. What time is brunch?"

"Eleven."

He was already starting toward his cottage. Over his shoulder he called, "I'll pick you up at ten forty-five."

Chapter 6

Still shaken by his kiss, Courtney seemed to be moving in a fog. She couldn't recall unlocking the door, snapping on the light, or climbing the stairs to her apartment. When she reached the top she was halfway across the room when she noticed the jumble of books on the floor.

"What...?" She turned and saw that her cabinet doors were lying open, books and papers scattered everywhere.

She dashed to her bedroom, only to find the same thing. The bookshelves had been swept of their books, which lay tumbled across her bed and floor.

She dug out her cell phone and dialed. By the time she reached the police department, her voice was shaking.

"This is Courtney Brennan. My apartment above my shop, Treasures, has been vandalized."

Though it seemed an eternity, the patrol car rolled up within minutes. Police Chief Boyd Thompson found Courtney standing in the doorway, looking pale and shaken.

A second car pulled up behind his. The mayor stepped out.

At the police chief's questioning look Wade Bentley said, "I was at city hall when I heard. Thought I'd see what was up."

Chief Thompson turned to Courtney. "Have you checked your shop?"

She nodded. "The door was locked. The security alarm was still armed."

"How about your apartment? Was the lock jimmied?"

"I think so."

"You think?" He moved past her and checked the lock. "How'd you get in? Was the door open, or did you need a key?"

"I…wasn't paying enough attention. But now I realize the door was unlocked."

Boyd glanced at her sharply. "You been drinking, Courtney?"

"Of course not. I was…distracted."

He nodded toward the rear cottage, where his deputy could be seen standing on the front step with Blair. "So was Colby, it seems. He was inside his cottage before he realized it'd been vandalized. His call came in within minutes of yours."

"Oh, no." Courtney clapped a hand to her mouth. "How bad is the damage?"

The police chief shrugged. "I haven't checked it out yet. Thought I'd start with you, then move on to Colby. Let's have a look at yours first."

With Courtney leading the way, he and the mayor followed her up the stairs to her apartment. "You touch anything?"

She shook her head.

"Good. I want my people to do a thorough exam before you clean up this mess."

Courtney looked around feeling sick at the thought of so many people going through her things. "You don't think this was just teen vandals?"

"I hope so. The fact that they avoided your shop is a good sign. Whoever did this didn't know enough about alarms to take a chance. But I take it as a personal insult that anyone in this town would think they can get away with this more than once." He patted her arm. "This is going to take a couple of hours, Courtney."

She nodded. "I understand." As he started away she said, "Would you mind if I went along with you to the Colby cottage?"

He shrugged. "Suit yourself. I have to assume, from the timing of your calls, that you and Colby were together tonight."

"That's right." Aware of the knowing looks that passed between the mayor and police chief, she trailed behind them as they walked across the backyard that separated her place from Blair's.

Inside, the vandalism was much more severe than hers had been.

"Oh, Blair." She felt such a wave of sadness at the sight of all his aunt's belongings littering the floor.

He touched a hand to her shoulder. "Detective Connell tells me that they got a call about your place, too. How bad was it?"

"Not as bad as this. But bad enough. The chief wants me to leave everything alone until his crew has had time to go over it."

"Same here."

Just then one of the police officers herded a young man and woman onto Blair's porch.

Courtney turned. "Kendra? What are you doing here?"

The young girl was holding tightly to her boyfriend's hand. "I don't know, Court. One minute Eddie and I were looking in the window of Treasures, and the next we were being hauled here."

The chief stepped out onto the porch. "What were you doing hanging around Ms. Brennan's shop at this hour?"

The girl looked helplessly at Courtney before explaining. "We were walking through town with our ice cream, and I wanted to show my boyfriend one of those goofy gargoyles we have in the shop window. If the light hits it a certain way, you can see its heart beating."

"Uh-huh." Chief Thompson was studying Eddie's spiked hair and fringed cowboy jacket. "You sure you didn't want to do more than look?"

Kendra glanced from the police chief to Courtney. "What's that supposed to mean? Court, we were just passing by and—"

Courtney turned to the chief. "Kendra works for me."

"Uh-huh." He pinned the two young people

with a stare meant to intimidate. "Kind of late to be window shopping. Do your folks know where you are?"

Though Kendra's eyes widened, she tossed her head with what she hoped was a look of defiance. "Are you going to arrest us?"

Chief Thompson gave a hiss of disgust. "Not tonight. But my officer will take your names and home phone numbers. And if everything you said doesn't check out, your folks will be hearing from me."

Courtney watched as the police officer led the two young people to a squad car, where he began writing. Because she couldn't bear to see the vandalism, she remained on the porch with Blair.

After following the police officers through the rooms of the cottage, the mayor stepped out onto the porch. "Chief Thompson says they'll be a couple of hours. I told him I'd be taking the two of you to the Daisy Diner. I'm sure some coffee would be welcome."

Courtney was shaking her head. "That's not necessary, Wade."

"I know it's not. But it's the least I can do." With his hand beneath her elbow he began steering her toward his car, with Blair reluctantly following.

As they settled into the back seat, Blair closed a hand over Courtney's. "You okay?"

"Fine. You?"

"Other than being mad as hell?"

That brought a smile to her lips. "Yeah. I know the feeling."

"I can see kids vandalizing an empty cottage, but now that it's obviously occupied, I don't get it. What's the fascination about Sarah's cottage?"

Courtney shook her head. "I don't have a clue. And why my place? And why now? In the year I've been here, this is the first time anything like this has happened."

The mayor, watching them in the rearview mirror, drove along the darkened streets until he parked in front of the cozy diner. Inside they were greeted with the sizzle and snap of burgers and the comforting smell of onions on the grill.

As soon as they were seated in a booth Carrie Lester hurried over to take their order.

"Hi, Courtney. Mayor Bentley." She stared pointedly at Blair. "You Sarah Colby's nephew?"

He looked surprised. "How did you know?"

She merely laughed. "Not too many secrets in Devil's Cove. What'll you have?"

"Just coffee, please."

"Same for me," Courtney added.

"Make it three," Wade Bentley told her.

"Right." Carrie hurried away and returned minutes later with their coffee.

As she poured, Courtney caught her hand to admire the glittering diamond ring that adorned the third finger of her left hand. "Prentice has excellent taste. In diamonds and women. Congratulations, Carrie."

"Thanks." The young woman hesitated. "Everyone's been so nice. I was afraid…"

"Of what?" The mayor demanded.

She shrugged, her cheeks growing pink. "That some folks might not approve of Prentice marrying a waitress from the Daisy Diner."

"That's silly." Courtney placed a hand over Carrie's. "You two make the perfect couple. He's only been in love with you since high school."

"I know. Isn't that just the sweetest thing?" She ducked her head and hurried away.

When she was gone, Wade Bentley cleared his throat. "A shame about these vandals. Not a very nice welcome for Sarah Colby's kin."

Blair shrugged. "I suppose it's a sign of the times. There's no getting away from crime anymore."

The mayor turned to Courtney. "You think it

could have been those two kids the police stopped?''

Courtney bit her lip. ''I can't believe it of Kendra. I think she and her boyfriend were just in the wrong place at the wrong time.''

''I hope you're right.'' The mayor studied Blair over the rim of his cup. ''You sure you don't have something somebody wants?''

Blair's head came up. ''Like what?''

Wade stirred more sugar into his coffee and tasted. ''Maybe Sarah left something of value.''

''Other than the land and her little cottage, which she acquired more than fifty years ago, my aunt left nothing of value that I know of.''

''How can you be sure? Maybe she had a few skeletons in her closet.''

''Aunt Sarah?'' Blair laughed. ''She may have been tough and stern, but she lived her life to a high moral code. She was the most righteous woman I've ever known.''

The mayor gave a grunt that might have been agreement or disapproval. ''She was tough. And efficient. Kept records of everything. My father used to say she kept better records than the FBI.'' He lowered his voice and he looked around to make certain no one could overhear him. ''That's what makes me think she might have left something that somebody would want."

"You mean like some sort of written documents?"

"Or letters. Maybe a journal. Do you know if she kept one?"

Blair frowned. "When I was a boy she used to write regularly in something she called her journal. I don't know if it was a personal diary, or just a log of things she wanted to remember. It was some sort of leather-bound ledger. But I haven't seen it in years. When I was here for the funeral, it wasn't among her papers."

The mayor leaned closer. "Maybe she put it into storage for safekeeping."

Blair thought a moment before shaking his head. "If she had, she'd have left a record of it. It was plain that she'd known for some time that she was dying, because she had everything in order and properly filed with her law firm. If she still had the ledger, I'm sure it would have been with her other documents. If you knew my aunt, you'd know that she was a stickler for records."

The mayor nodded thoughtfully. "Unless it contained things she didn't want to become public knowledge. Then she might have decided to conceal it."

Blair sipped. "What would be the point of writing something unless she expected it to be read?"

When Carrie approached with the pot of coffee to offer refills, Courtney refused. "Thanks, Carrie." She turned to Wade Bentley. "I really need to get back now."

Blair nodded in agreement. "I'm sure by now the police will have done what they needed to do."

The three exited the diner and drove the entire way back in silence. When they reached Courtney's shop, Chief Thompson was standing with his deputies by the back door.

He walked over to the mayor's car and leaned in the open window. "No prints. Looks like they wore gloves."

Blair sat forward. "So it wasn't just teens passing by and looking for a little fun."

"It doesn't appear to be. But I'll be darned if I can figure out what this is about. It's almost as if somebody was systematically searching for something." He fixed Blair with a look. "You have any ideas about this?"

Blair gave a sigh. "The mayor just asked the same thing. But I don't have any answers."

As he and Courtney climbed out of the mayor's car, the chief stepped back. "Okay. Try to get some sleep. If you think of something, anything, no matter how trivial, give me a call.''

''I will, Chief.'' Blair watched as the mayor drove away, followed by the police chief and his deputies.

When they were alone, he turned to Courtney. ''Come on. I'll go inside with you.''

''There's no need to do that.'' She stepped inside, her hand on the door.

Before she could close it in his face he swept past her. ''Humor me.''

Leaving her no time to argue, he led the way up the stairs and studied the mess. Without a word he began picking up the books and magazines that had been strewn across the floor.

''Blair, it's late. I can do that in the morning.''

He turned to her with a look that said, more than words, that he wasn't about to be swayed from his mission.

With a sigh she took the items from his hands and began returning them to shelves and cabinets. In less than an hour the apartment had been restored to order.

''Now try to get some sleep, Courtney.''

As he started toward the stairs, she stopped him with a hand on his arm. ''Sorry. Now it's your turn.''

At his arched brow she picked up her keys. "What's sauce for the goose..."

"It's late."

"That was my line, remember?" She strode ahead of him and held the door, then locked it when he stepped outside. Pocketing the keys, she closed a hand around his arm and moved along beside him as they picked their way in the darkness.

When they reached his cottage, she couldn't hold back the little gasp at the mess, made worse by the police investigation. It was so much worse than hers had been. Without a word she began gathering up the books and handing them to him as he replaced them on shelves.

When they'd finished in the living room they moved on to the bedroom.

"So many books," she said with a sigh as she began picking them up.

"They were my aunt's passion. I can't remember a single day when she wasn't reading. Except when she was writing in that ledger."

"You said that's when you used to go exploring."

He accepted another armload of books from her and began arranging them on a shelf. "Yeah. Aunt

Sarah used to get so lost in her journal, she wouldn't miss me for hours.''

Courtney paused. ''Where did she keep it?''

He pointed to the small desk across the room. ''That's where she used to sit when she was writing in it. But I don't recall ever seeing it lying around.''

''Curious. Maybe she kept it in one of the desk drawers.''

He shrugged. ''Maybe. I wouldn't know. I never went through my aunt's things when I was a boy.''

''What about now? Have you looked for it?''

Blair shook his head. ''Until the mayor mentioned it, I'd forgotten all about that journal.'' Though he looked skeptical, he opened both desk drawers, finding them empty.

He glanced over at Courtney. ''You don't really think somebody would go to all this trouble for an old diary, do you?''

''You said yourself that Sarah spent a lot of time writing in it. Could there be something in that journal that might prove embarrassing for someone?''

''I don't know. But since the place was ransacked before I even got here, the thieves would have had plenty of opportunity to find it and destroy it, if that's what they were after. So why would they come back for another look?''

''Why, indeed? Unless they didn't find it the first time, and thought you might have brought it with you.''

Blair swore under his breath. ''I hope you're right.''

She looked at him in surprise. ''Why?''

''Because if that's the case, now that they've had a second look, they have to know that there is no journal. And maybe they'll leave this place alone.''

He glanced at the clock on the nightstand. ''It's nearly three in the morning. Come on. I'll walk you back.''

As they started across the yard he dropped an arm around her shoulders. When she didn't flinch he found himself smiling. ''Maybe some good can come from this after all.''

''What's that supposed to mean?''

''You don't find me as repulsive as you did when we first met.''

''How do you know?''

''You didn't push me away just then.''

''Maybe I'm just too tired.''

''Maybe.'' They paused outside her door. He

tipped up her chin. "Mind if I try an experiment?"

Before she could reply he lowered his mouth to hers and kissed her, long and slow and deep.

When he finally lifted his head to stare down into her eyes, his voice was rough. "It just happened again."

"What happened?"

"The ground tilted. The sky revolved. One kiss, and my whole world turned upside down. The last time, I was so confused, I was halfway inside my cottage before I realized it had been vandalized."

She managed a quick laugh. "You poor baby." She laid a hand on his cheek. "You really need to get some sleep."

His hands tightened at her shoulders, and he dragged her close before again taking her mouth with his. This time, as his lips moved over hers, she gave a sudden intake of breath before feeling her head spin. Needs she hadn't even known existed simmered just below the surface, threatening to scald her. She clutched blindly at his waist and held on as he pressed her back against the door and kissed her until she was trembling.

When at last he drew a little away, he watched her struggle for breath.

His voice was deep with suppressed passion.

"Maybe what we both need is sleep. But I'd sleep a whole lot better if you'd invite me up to share your bed."

"Sorry." She couldn't believe how hard it was to speak. "I sleep alone."

"Too bad. It could have been memorable." He gave her one last smoldering glance before turning away.

She waited until her hands had stopped shaking before attempting to unlock her door. All the way up the stairs she chided herself for being so hasty. Maybe a memorable night with Blair would have been just the thing to chase away the lingering fears from the break-in.

Still, she didn't think her heart was ready for another battering. Especially if the night proved to be a little too...memorable. The better choice would be to keep on avoiding him until his job here was done. When Blair Colby left Devil's Cove, as she knew he would, she wanted no regrets. And no more heartache.

Chapter 7

Blair carried his coffee outside and was treated to the sight of a family of ducks swimming by as he settled himself on the end of the dock. He'd expected to sleep late, and was still cursing his inner clock for waking him so early. Not that he minded, given the view. He found himself charmed by the gentle lap of water against the shore, the croak of bullfrogs, the shadow of a huge turtle cruising just below the surface.

Far out on the lake were the morning fishermen, casting their lines, dreaming of the big catch. On the horizon were the familiar white sails as sailboats danced across the waves.

It was a scene he'd carried in his heart since boyhood. Summer in Devil's Cove. Here, despite his aunt's stern rules and no-nonsense approach to life, he'd found refuge from the regimen of tough private schools, and a reprieve from the constant tug-of-war between his parents. After a lifetime of soul-searching, he'd come to terms with the battleground that had been their marriage. He'd accepted each of them and their many spouses with, if not love, at least affection. Still, the scars remained. He shied away from long-term relationships. Whenever a woman started thinking about a white gown and happily-ever-after, he preferred to wave to her image in his rearview mirror. He didn't mean to be cynical. But it was only fair to a woman to admit that constancy wasn't a Colby trait, considering his gene pool.

Was that why his aunt had never married? She'd never talked to him about his parents, nor, he realized, about herself. It occurred to him that he never really knew his aunt Sarah at all. She'd kept her secrets to herself, revealing nothing to the boy to whom she opened her home but never her heart.

What was it she'd written in that journal? If her daily discipline had been any indication, she'd been driven to fill the pages. But with what? From the little he'd seen of her life, it had been one of dull routine.

Still, she was, he supposed, well positioned to write the history of Devil's Cove. After retiring as secretary to the governor, she'd served as secretary to the Library Association, the Chamber of Commerce, the Zoning Board and the City Council. There were few in town she didn't know personally. And because of her quiet way of listening, many of those who knew her even slightly found themselves opening up to her. That would have given her ample opportunity to learn a great many secrets. But the very private woman he knew wouldn't have been comfortable writing such things in a journal and leaving it behind for all to read.

Blair rubbed a hand over his face and drained his coffee. As he got to his feet and started toward the cottage, he caught sight of Courtney on her upper balcony, watering her plants. She was wearing some sort of long, opaque gown that revealed the outline of her body in the rays of sunlight spilling across the railing. Her hair fell long and loose in a mass of tangles.

Another reason, he thought, to be grateful for that damn inner clock. He wouldn't have missed this view for the world. He might not have any long-term plans for Courtney Brennan, but that didn't stop him from enjoying the thrill of the chase. Especially when the prey was as smart as she was beautiful. That only made the hunt that much more exciting.

"Good morning." At Blair's knock Courtney opened the door and stepped outside carrying her sea bag and wearing a long silk skirt and matching top in sea-foam green. Her hair was plaited in a fat braid that fell over one breast.

Blair took a moment to drink in the sight of her. "I hope brunch isn't formal."

"Not at all. You look fine." And he did, in charcoal pants and a lighter gray silk tee. His hair, she noted, was still damp from the shower.

He gave her another long, steady look. "And you're gorgeous."

His unexpected compliment had her pulse jumping as he held the door to his car. Or maybe it was the possessive brush of his hand along her arm. Whatever the reason, she took several calming breaths and had her heartbeat settled down to its normal rhythm by the time he'd turned the key in the ignition.

He glanced over as they headed along the street.

''Did you alert your family to what happened last night?''

She shook her head. ''It would only cause them all to lose sleep. I am hoping, though, to speak with Poppie, whenever I can get him alone.''

''You don't think he'll worry?''

''He will. That can't be helped. But he has a wonderfully logical mind that might be able to see what the authorities are missing.'' She turned to study Blair's profile. ''If he wants to talk to you, would you mind?''

''Of course not. I'll do whatever it takes to get to the bottom of this. When it happened once, I was willing to accept teen vandals. But twice?'' He frowned. ''That's pushing it.''

Courtney expelled the breath she hadn't even been aware she was holding. ''I'm glad you feel that way. Because it's what bothered me all night.''

He touched a hand to hers. Just a touch, but she felt the warmth of it all the way up her arm. ''I'm really sorry, Courtney. I don't know what's happening, but somehow I feel responsible.''

''It isn't your fault.''

He glanced over. ''You said yourself that this never happened before I moved in.''

"That doesn't mean it's your fault. You certainly didn't invite the trouble."

He grinned. "Did I just hear you defend me?"

She arched a brow. "A momentary lapse. I'm sure I'll recover my senses any minute now."

"Admit it. I'm starting to get to you."

"So are the mosquitoes. That's why I brought along my repellant."

"So that's what you've been using? Man repellant?"

"Is it working?"

He shot her a sidelong glance. "What do you think?"

They were both laughing as he drove up the long curving driveway of The Willows, where several other cars were already parked. As they walked around to the patio, they could hear the quiet hum of voices, and the high, shrill laughter of Danny and T.J.

The two little boys were picking tomatoes from Poppie's garden, under the watchful eye of Hannah, who was holding a basket to collect their treasures. Ethan and Jason were standing by the grill with Frank, who was wielding his tongs like a Samurai as he flipped chunks of beef and ham and turkey.

Sidney was arranging lush flowers and foliage

in crystal vases, while Emily and Bert were busy setting out place mats on the glass-topped table.

Charley stepped out of the kitchen with a pitcher of juice. "Oh, good, Courtney. We were hoping you'd finish setting the table. You always make it so much prettier than any of us."

"Uh-huh." Courtney nudged Blair. "In Brennan language that means they're running late this morning and hope I'll pitch in."

He grinned. "I'll help. Just tell me where everything is."

"Dishes, flatware and such in the kitchen. Trudy's domain," she said under her breath. "Come on. Might as well get it over with. Then we can feast."

Inside, Trudy looked up from the oven, where she was removing a pan of rolls. "About time you got here. We need you to..."

"...set the table," Courtney finished for her. "Blair said he'll help."

"He'd better, if he wants to eat." Trudy set down the pan and reached for a second one.

As she did, Blair walked over and breathed in the perfume of cinnamon. "This smells heavenly."

"That's what they all say." Trudy broke off a steaming piece of biscuit and handed it to him.

"Men have been known to beg me to marry them, just so they can have my recipe."

Blair chewed, swallowed, then dropped on one knee in front of the old woman. "Very smart men. But not nearly worthy of you, Trudy. I, on the other hand, will treat you like the queen of the kitchen you obviously are, if you'll do me the honor."

"Save it, honey." She gave a throaty laugh. "Better men than you have tried and failed. But since you went to all that trouble, I'll see that you get an extra cinnamon roll with brunch."

"You're an angel of mercy." He straightened and picked up the armload of dishes Courtney was holding out to him.

"I should have warned you. Trudy has her own man repellant."

"Yeah. I noticed. But the old Colby charm can break through."

"Don't hold your breath, Prince Charming." She led the way to the patio.

Once outside, Blair was soon caught up in the weekly ritual. This was, he realized, much more than a meal. Each member of the Brennan family seemed to have a part to play, each using a particular skill that added to the overall charm of the event. Hannah and the little boys sliced fresh tomatoes from the garden onto a lovely white platter. Then Danny and T.J. carried it ever so carefully to the table, where they stood beaming with pride. Emily was busy mixing equal parts of champagne and orange juice like a chemist. Sidney and Courtney fussed over the table arrangements, moving vases of flowers until they were exactly to their liking, before adding pretty cushions to the surrounding chairs and chaises. Charley assisted Trudy, rolling out a cart of breads and rolls from the kitchen, while Bert, her cap of white curls dancing in the breeze, moved among them like a military general.

Seeing that Blair's chore was successfully completed, Bert caught his arm. "Now that you've helped with the table, why don't you snag two of those mimosas and join me on the glider."

He picked up two long-stemmed tulip glasses of frothy orange juice and champagne and handed one to her before sitting down beside her, enjoying the gentle motion of the glider.

"Thank you for inviting me to join your family, Mrs. Brennan."

"It's Bert. And I hope you don't find us too overwhelming."

"I suppose I did at first glance. But now I've managed to sort you all out."

"Good. That's the hardest part. Now I hope you'll just relax and enjoy the show." She nodded toward her husband, who was beginning to remove the meats from the grill onto a platter. "Frank loves his Sunday brunch with the family."

"I can see why."

She turned to study him. "Do you have brothers or sisters?"

He shook his head. "I'm an only."

"So was our Christopher."

Blair tried to hide his surprise at her statement. "It must have been hard to lose your son."

"It was. But look at the lovely legacy he left us." She sipped her drink. "I knew your aunt Sarah."

He laughed. "I guess just about everybody in Devil's Cove knew her."

Bert nodded. "I remember you, too, from your summers with her. Not well, of course. But I recall seeing you with her a time or two."

"I suppose you were wondering how a stern old spinster like Sarah Colby could cope with her brother's son."

Bert smiled. "Not at all. After fifty years of teaching, I learned that none of us is what we seem on the outside. I always thought that Sarah's stern demeanor hid a tender heart. One that was probably broken by cruelty or carelessness. I thought perhaps the sad little boy who spent his summers with her was here to heal as much as to be healed.''

"You thought I was sad?''

She smiled. "Weren't you?''

He nodded. "Very. But I guess I wasn't aware that it showed.''

Frank strolled over to the glider. "You've had Bert's attention entirely too long, my boy. Now it's my turn.'' He helped his wife to her feet and tucked her arm through his.

As they walked away, looking for all the world like young lovers, Blair trailed slowly behind, mulling the older woman's words. He'd never before considered the fact that his presence here each summer might have comforted a lonely old woman, but he hoped it was so.

At the table Blair held Courtney's chair before taking the seat beside her.

She leaned close. "You and my grandmother looked cozy.''

"She's a remarkable woman.''

Courtney smiled. "You don't know the half of it.''

From her position at the end of the table, Bert watched her granddaughter lost in quiet conversation with Blair Colby and gave a little cat smile of satisfaction.

Chapter 8

"Goodbye, Aunt Courtney." Danny locked his chubby arms around her neck and gave her a sticky kiss, which she warmly returned, before doing the same with his little brother, T.J.

After a leisurely brunch, following by a raucous game of croquet on the rolling lawn, in which everyone participated, there had been a second, lighter meal and plenty of time for family conversation. Now the little boys and their parents were heading home, which signaled the end of the entertaining Sunday for the entire family.

Courtney and Blair walked with her sisters and their husbands to their cars.

Seeing Jason Cooper climbing behind the wheel of Blair's car, Courtney turned to him with a look of surprise. "Where is he going?"

"Back to my place. Emily offered to follow him there and take him home after he delivers my car in the driveway."

"How are you planning on getting back?"

He shot her a wicked grin. "With you. Aboard your sailboat. I think it's time I brush up on my sailing skills." Seeing the way her lips pursed, he couldn't help adding, "Are you pouting because I didn't ask you first?"

"I'm not pouting. I never pout. But I do think you could have asked before assuming you could ride along in my boat."

"Fair's fair. I took you home in my car last night, didn't I?"

"That's different. You had no choice. It was storming."

He pointed to the clear, cloudless sky. "Looks like a perfect night to sail home. And if you decide you don't want to go straight home, and we anchor in some romantic little cove for a midnight swim, I promise not to complain or charge you with harassment."

"You're too good to be true."

"That's me." His smile went straight to her heart. "Practically a saint."

Beside them her grandparents chuckled at the good-natured banter between these two, and waved until the rest of their family was out of sight.

When they turned toward the house, Bert tucked an arm through her husband's. "If you don't mind, I think I'll walk off some of that fine food along the shore. Maybe you could take Courtney and Blair inside where it's cooler."

Frank kissed his wife's cheek and watched her walk away before inviting the two inside.

As they stepped into the kitchen, Trudy fished a pack of cigarettes from her apron pocket and ducked out onto the patio. Knowing how much the judge disapproved of her habit, she passed him without a word. He did the same as he led Courtney and Blair through the kitchen, where the dishwasher was humming, and along the cool, tiled hallway until they reached his office. Once inside he settled himself at his desk and waited until they'd chosen adjoining chairs before speaking.

"You wanted to tell me something, Courtney."

She nodded. "How did Bert know?"

He merely smiled. "After a lifetime together, people generally read each other's minds and moods. She sensed that you two young people wanted some time alone with me." He clasped his hands on the desktop, steepling his fingers. "My time is yours."

As simply as possible Courtney told him about the break-ins.

When she was finished the judge asked, "What does Chief Thompson think?"

"He assumed the first break-in was teen vandals. Now he's not so sure. Mostly, he seemed insulted that someone could get away with such a thing in his town not once, but twice. Mayor Bentley seemed to share his reaction, and wondered whether someone might be looking for something specific."

"The mayor? When did you talk to him?"

"He arrived right behind the police chief. He was kind enough to take us out for coffee while the police finished their investigation." Courtney glanced at Blair. "We didn't want to worry you, Poppie. But I told Blair that I needed to have your take on this. You've sat in on enough trials to have a handle on the criminal mind. Are we missing something here?"

The older man tapped a finger on the desktop. "I'm inclined to agree with the chief that a single incident could be random, but a second one can't be treated as cavalierly.'' He turned to Blair. ''Do you have any enemies?''

Blair shook his head. ''None that I know of.''

''Any idea what this could be about?''

Blair gave an exasperated sigh. ''The more I think about it, the more questions I have. My aunt was a simple woman who lived a simple life. Besides, the vandals had ample time to search the cottage before I moved in. Why would they need a second break-in?''

''If they're actually searching for something specific, and didn't find it earlier, they could believe you had possession of it and may have brought it with you when you moved in.''

Blair sighed. ''That's pretty much what the mayor hinted. But after my aunt's death, I was notified by her law firm that they were in possession of all her legal documents. I didn't go over them myself, but the firm seemed to think they were the usual things. Birth certificate. Proof of purchase of the land where she lived, as well as old tax records. I'm certain they would have notified me if they'd found anything out of the ordinary. So far the law firm hasn't reported anything unusual. I can assure you that the only things I brought with me were clothes and a few bath and bed linens. Certainly nothing worth trashing the cottage for.''

Courtney interrupted. ''And what of my apartment, Poppie? Why would someone target my place?''

''Proximity to Blair, I suspect.'' He smiled gently at his granddaughter. ''This is a small town, Courtney. Once you and Blair are seen together, there are some who may believe that you're sharing more than a sailboat ride.''

''I resent that.''

''You may resent it, but it's a fact of life here in Devil's Cove.'' He held up a hand to still her protest. ''What may be nothing more than an innocent good-night kiss between the two of you could be misconstrued as much more by someone watching under the cover of darkness.''

The words she'd been about to speak died on her lips. The mere thought of someone watching them, stalking them, left her chilled.

Her grandfather came around the desk and took her hands in his. ''I'd like you to consider coming back to The Willows for a few weeks. Just until the police find out what's going on.''

She was already shaking her head. ''I can't come running home every time I hear bumps in the night.''

"This is a lot more than mere bumps, sweetheart. You have to know that this is serious."

"I do, Poppie. But I won't be forced out of my own place by vandals. Besides, if, as you suggest, we're being watched, it's pretty obvious that our stalkers prefer striking when we're away."

"That's true. For now. But if they were to become bolder, they might decide to strike while you're there."

She took a deep breath. "I won't deny that I'm afraid. But I won't be driven away by fear."

He squeezed her hands. "I guess I expected that from you. I don't want you to be alarmed, Courtney, but you can't afford to take any chances. Until this is resolved, you must remain aware and alert at all times."

She nodded. "I will, Poppie. Promise."

"Good girl." He drew her up and pressed a kiss to her cheek. "Now go and find your grandmother and tell her it's safe to come inside. We're done with our discussion."

As Blair got to his feet and started to follow her, Frank Brennan placed a hand on his arm, holding him back. When they were alone, his manner turned grave. "I intend to speak with Chief Thompson first thing in the morning. Until then, I hope you'll find a way to see that my granddaughter isn't alone.''

When the meaning of those words struck him, Blair shot the old man an incredulous look. ''If you're asking me to spend the night with Courtney, I think I'd better warn you that your granddaughter has a mind of her own. And that mind is very resistant to any sort of relationship with me.''

''I'm not surprised.'' The old man chuckled. ''She's just like her grandmother. It took all my powers of persuasion to win that woman's heart. But it was certainly worth the effort. From what I've observed, you're not immune to my granddaughter's charms. Nor she to yours.''

''I won't deny it. But it's a little early in the game...''

Frank lowered his voice when he heard the sound of footsteps drawing close. ''I'm not suggesting you sleep with Courtney, son. In fact, I'd hope that you could avoid that particular temptation for the moment. Her tender heart is very important to me. Just see that she isn't alone for this one night. After that, I'll do my best to arrange for nightly police patrols. Without her knowledge, of course.''

''If she finds out what you've suggested, it'll

be your head she comes after. Right after she cuts off mine, of course.''

The old man winked. ''Don't I know it?''

When Courtney and her grandmother stepped into the room, the two men were standing a little apart, wearing matching looks of innocence. Which only served to alert both women to the fact that these two men were undoubtedly guilty of something.

''Thank you again for the lovely day.'' Blair, shoes in hand, pants rolled to his knees, stood on shore and offered a kiss to Bert and a handshake to Frank.

After kissing her grandparents, Courtney, who had stripped off her more formal clothes to reveal a sea-foam-green bikini underneath, picked up her sea bag and started wading through the water toward the little sailboat anchored offshore.

After climbing aboard, Courtney stowed her gear and began to unfurl the sails. ''Okay, mate. Time for that refresher course. Think you can handle the anchor?''

In reply Blair leaned his weight into the chain, drawing it up until the anchor was aboard.

As the breeze began filling the sails, Courtney manned the tiller and the main sheets while Blair easily handled the jib. Within minutes the little craft was skimming the waves.

He glanced over, loving the way she looked, feet planted, hair streaming out behind her. With moonlight trailing a path of gold across the water, she more resembled an ethereal mermaid than a flesh-and-blood female.

"You should be glad to have me aboard. Isn't this a lot of work for just one person to handle?"

She shook her head. "After all these years, it's second nature. But I have to admit it's nice to have someone to share the chores." Still holding the tiller, she sat down and drew a beach towel around her shoulders. "Now that the hard work is behind us, it should be smooth sailing home."

After securing the lines he crossed the deck and settled himself beside her. "You sure you want to head home so soon?" He glanced up at the stars, looking so big and bright in the darkened sky, that it felt as though he could reach up and touch them. "Seems a shame to waste such a rare night as this on a short sail home."

"What did you have in mind?"

He dropped an arm around her shoulders. "I didn't bother to bring along trunks. But if you happened to find a deserted stretch of beach, I wouldn't object to skinny-dipping."

She gave him a mocking laugh, even while her heart did a quick somersault. "Ever the hero."

He gave a casual shrug of his shoulders. "Okay. If you object to my naked body beside yours in the water, I'll stay in the boat and just watch you." He allowed his gaze to skim her from head to toe. "It'll be a tough job, but I'm up to it."

"You never give up, do you?"

"That's what makes me a hero."

"Okay, hero, what were you and Poppie up to when Bert and I walked into the office?"

"Up to?" He slanted her a look. "Can't two men have a manly discussion without women becoming all uptight about it?"

"It's been my experience that most manly discussions focus on women."

"Now, how could you possibly be in a position to know that? I'll remind you that once a woman enters the discussion it's no longer manly."

"So, which were you were discussing? Hunting, shooting, spitting or swearing?"

"That just shows how little you know about men, my sweet. We could have been talking about the best way to grill salmon, or how to prevent slugs on the tomatoes."

"Or what to do about Courtney until these vandals are caught."

"What's that?" He cupped a hand to his ear. "Do I hear muttering from one of the crew?"

"It's my ship, which means I'm the captain. You're the crew. And I know Poppie too well. He looked like the cat that swallowed the canary."

"I'm shocked at your suspicious mind. Shocked, I tell you." Keeping his arm around her shoulders, he slid his other hand around her waist and lowered his head to hers.

"Now what're you up to?"

With his mouth inches from hers he whispered, "Looks like I'm going to have to do something drastic to stop this mutiny."

Chapter 9

The instant his mouth closed over hers, Courtney felt her heart do a strange dip. The words she'd been about to speak were forgotten. As was the tiller. Though her hand remained firmly clenched around it, she wasn't aware of anything except the slow pitch and roll of the boat, and the wild thundering of her heartbeat. Her emotions, always so carefully in check, began to slip free, leaving her feeling strangely disoriented.

Instead of releasing her he took the kiss deeper. Somehow her arms found their way around his neck and she held on as he took her on the most incredible ride. While his lips teased hers, his hands moved along her bare flesh, burning a trail of fire wherever they touched. And, oh, how they touched her. Boldly. Like a man starved for the touch of her.

When at last he lifted his head, it was to run hot, wet kisses down her throat to the spot where her pulse was pounding like a jackhammer.

''Still feeling mutinous?''

She managed a shaky laugh. ''I'm not sure I'd care to share with you what I'm feeling just now.''

He nuzzled her neck. ''I'll share if you do.''

''Okay.'' She brought her hands to his chest to push him a little away. ''You go first.''

''Think you're sly, don't you? All right. I'll share.'' He paused for just a moment. ''I'm feeling just a little bit dazed. As though I ought to know what to do next, but can't quite figure it out. Like a man standing before a banquet, and eager for the feast, but afraid to admit just how hungry I am or it will all be taken away. You dazzle me, Courtney. And you scare me.'' He took hold of her hands and pressed a kiss to each palm, all the while staring into her eyes.

She yanked them away as though burned. ''Don't do that.''

There was just the slightest catch in her voice

that alerted him there was more here than passion. Was that panic in her eyes? Pain?

"Do what?"

"Play me like this." She fisted her hands in her lap to keep him from taking them again. "It's all a game to you, isn't it?"

"What?"

"The chase. Romancing the girl. Getting her into your bed. Another notch on your belt."

He hadn't moved. And yet she could feel him assessing her.

When he finally spoke his voice was a little too cool. And far too controlled. "Who did this to you?"

"Did what?"

"Hurt you so badly you refuse to trust your own feelings."

"I'm not feeling anything except foolish for falling for such a tired line as yours." She gathered the beach towel around her, struggling with her dignity. "We've blown off course."

"It doesn't matter. We'll find our way home. We're close enough to shore to see exactly where we are. I'm more concerned about us."

"There is no us, Blair. We're nothing more than neighbors. If one of us wants it to be more, that's too bad, because the other has already been to that playground before.''

''Pretty rough play. It's left you bloody and bruised.''

''But alive, thank you. Older but wiser.''

''Is that what you're calling cynicism these days? Wisdom? What happens when someone finds a chink in that wall you've built around your heart?''

''I'll add a few more bricks.''

''Oh, baby. He really did a number on you.'' Without warning he gathered her close and pressed his lips to a tangle of hair at her temple.

She would have been able to fight him if there had been fire in his eyes, or a hint of fury in his tone. She'd anticipated a duel, or at least a display of arrogance on his part. But this unexpected tenderness was her undoing.

''Don't.'' She breathed the word against his chest, ashamed to feel moisture on her lashes, on her cheeks. She never cried. Never.

As his mouth moved over her closed eyes, her cheek, the tip of her nose, kissing away all trace of tears, her feeble protest was lost in a shaky sigh that seemed to rise up from the very depths of her soul.

She found herself waiting hungrily for his lips

to claim hers. When they didn't, she opened her eyes, searching his face.

He was watching her with an expression she didn't recognize.

Without a word she lifted her face to his and offered her mouth. For the space of a heartbeat he remained perfectly still, as though fighting the desire to take what she was offering.

When at last his arms tightened around her, she made a little purr of approval. And then his mouth covered hers in a kiss of such intensity it caught them both by surprise.

"I've wanted this. Just this." His words were spoken inside her mouth as he drew out the kiss, while his hands, those strong, clever hands, moved over her.

He couldn't seem to stop kissing her. Each time he came up for air, he had the desperate need to take her mouth again, afraid it would be the last.

He'd never known a woman's taste to be this intoxicating. As clean and fresh as the cool water of Lake Michigan that glistened in the moonlight around them. And the feel of her in his arms. Had any other woman's body been this perfect? All that flawless skin, kissed by the sun, and so soft to the touch she seemed almost otherworldly. He couldn't seem to get enough of her. He wanted to simply devour her.

He plunged his hands into the tangles of her hair, loving the feel of it against his palms. It was even softer than he'd imagined. He pressed his face to it, breathing in the fragrance that reminded him of evergreen after a spring rain.

"You feel so good. And taste even better." His mouth moved over hers, and this time she returned his kisses with equal fervor, all trace of reluctance gone. He could sense the loneliness, the longing, that flowed from her, and spoke to an equal longing inside him that he hadn't even known was there. The realization startled him.

And then he remembered how hurt she'd been. How wounded.

With his hands on her shoulders he eased back. "I need…" A cold swim, he thought. Aloud he merely said, "…to breathe. We both do."

She couldn't hide the hurt in her eyes. In her voice. After breaking through her resistance, was he rejecting her?

"All right." She could feel her lungs straining, as though she'd been sailing through a storm. In a way, maybe she had.

"We could anchor somewhere and go for a swim."

She shook her head, feeling oddly deflated. "It's too late. And, as you said, you've no trunks. I think I'd rather head home."

As she reached for the tiller he closed a hand over hers. "I need to say something."

She glanced over at him.

"It would have been easy to cross a line just now. We were both willing." Before she could interrupt he went on as quickly as possible, determined to explain. "I don't want you to think I stopped because I don't want you. I do." He rubbed a hand over his face. "Desperately, in fact. You were right about me, Courtney. Loyalty, constancy, those aren't traits that run in my family. In fact, the Colbys have a history of being pretty casual about love and marriage. That's why I vowed never to take that particular plunge." He lifted his hand away from hers. "Now you know. The last thing someone like you needs in her life is someone like me."

She hated the fact that she was shivering. It wasn't because of the cold truth he'd just shared with her, or the fact that he'd put a distance between them, both literally and figuratively. It was, quite simply, the night breeze on her bare flesh. At least, that was all she was willing to admit to.

Her voice was crisp. "Thanks for the warning."

Back on course, she thought as she turned the little craft toward the cove. She wouldn't leave herself open and vulnerable around him again. She might not appreciate his honesty at the moment, but she was certain that in time she'd be grateful. At least that's what she would cling to.

She stood, planting her feet as she prepared to anchor. "Can you handle that line?"

She was being entirely too cool, but he couldn't think of any way to repair the damage now. She'd deserved complete honesty, and that's what he'd given her. If it hurt, so be it. Better to be hurt now, before this went any further, than to wait and confess his shortcomings after they'd crossed a line.

He helped furl the sails and tossed the anchor over the side. As they slipped over the rail and started toward the dock, he put a hand on her arm and pointed.

A thin ribbon of light was moving around the perimeter of his cottage.

"Flashlight," she whispered.

He nodded and motioned for her to remain there while he hurried ashore.

Unwilling to stay behind, Courtney dashed

through the shallows and reached shore just behind Blair.

At the sound of their splashing, the light was
extinguished. All that could be seen was a shadowy figure dissolving abruptly into the darkness.
The only sound they heard was hurried footsteps
receding into the distance.

And then there was only silence, broken by the
gentle lap of water against the shore.

"We've taken a mold of the only shoe print we
could find." Chief Thompson watched as his deputies loaded gear into a squad car. "I'm sure, if
you hadn't come upon the intruder so quickly,
he'd have taken the time to erase that bit of evi-
dence before leaving. My deputies checked out
your place, Courtney, and found no sign of any
break-in. That means that he started here, with the
Colby cottage. No telling if he'd have moved on
to your place afterward."

The police chief watched as his deputies backed
out of the driveway. Their headlights illuminated
Blair's car, parked beside his cottage. "What worries me is that this guy didn't seem intimidated by
the presence of that car. He should have been
afraid that you'd be home and catch him."

"Unless," Blair said tiredly, "he watched Jason Cooper drive my car here and leave immediately afterward with his wife.''

Boyd Thompson nodded and clipped his flashlight to his belt. ''That's what has me so concerned. Our guy has to be stalking you.'' He sighed. ''With the limited manpower of our small-town police force, I can't promise you around-the-clock protection, but I'll do the best I can. In the meantime, I'd like the two of you to take precautions.''

Blair glanced at Courtney, who was looking entirely too pale. ''Do you know someone in town who can install a security alarm?''

''I do.'' The chief's voice was all business now. ''Along with motion-sensitive lights that will go on the minute anyone gets close to the building. If you'll give me a pad and pen, I'll write down the company name and number.''

As the police chief wrote on a notepad, Blair ran a hand through his hair, wondering just how, after that little scene in the boat, he was going to accommodate Frank Brennan and get Courtney to spend the night. He sighed. Even if he should succeed, how would he manage to keep his hands off her?

What a mess he'd made of things.

''Courtney.'' Chief Thompson turned to her.

"Would you like me to drive you to your grandparents' house?"

"Whatever for?"

He gave her an incredulous look. "You can't stay alone over there."

"In case you haven't noticed, Boyd, I'm a big girl now. I can't go running home to Bert and Poppie every time something goes wrong."

"Look." His tone hardened. "This isn't about running scared. This is about being sensible. Someone is going to a lot of trouble here. As an officer of the law, that says to me that someone is also growing desperate. And desperate people are dangerous people. I'd feel a lot better if you'd let me drive you to The Willows."

Courtney glanced at the kitchen clock on Blair's stove. "It's nearly four. I won't have you waking my grandparents at this time of the morning." She squared her shoulders. "Your deputies said there was no sign of entry at my place. I'm going home. At least I can have a hot shower and a little quiet time before I have to open my shop."

Boyd's frown remained as he glanced at his wristwatch. "Suit yourself, Courtney. If you're determined, I'll walk with you before I leave."

They said their good-nights to Blair and walked in silence to her shop.

At the door she turned to the police chief. "Thanks for everything, Boyd. I'm sorry you've had to put in so many long hours over this."

"Not nearly as sorry as that troublemaking son of a—" he caught himself "—as our vandal is going to be when we catch him." He sighed. "And we will catch him. It's just a matter of time." As she turned away he stopped her. "What do you know about Blair Colby?"

She shrugged. "Not much. But he has excellent credentials as an architect." She smiled. "And from what I've seen of him with my family, they seem to be growing fond of him."

"And you?"

She arched a brow.

He flushed. "Sorry. It's none of my business. But I'm automatically suspicious of anyone who brings trouble to my town. Just…be sensible and be cautious, Courtney."

She touched a hand to his arm. "Thanks, Boyd. That's what Poppie said to me earlier tonight."

She watched until the police chief settled into the squad car and drove away. Then, carefully locking her door, she made her way up the stairs above her shop to her apartment.

Sleep, she knew, would be impossible for what remained of this night.

Chapter 10

Courtney sat at her desk and opened a folder. After a long, perfumed bath to soothe her nerves, she'd slipped into a silk kimono, determined to use this last hour or so before dawn doing something constructive. Nothing like writing checks to take her mind off this latest trouble.

Her hand paused in midair. It wasn't the attempted break-in at Blair's cottage that kept distracting her. It was Blair.

She thought she'd had enough experience with men to be able to tell the difference between truth and lies. Between a simple statement and a smooth line. She didn't want to believe this man. But when he'd told her that unvarnished truth about his family and their lack of commitment, she'd seen something in his eyes. Pain. Very real and very deep. And it had spoken to the unresolved pain in her own heart.

She tapped the pen on her desktop. Why was she letting this man get to her? What did it matter if he was a good liar or an honest man? Her life was going just fine, thank you very much. A man would only complicate things. Especially one with baggage. Didn't she have enough of her own?

She forced herself back to the task at hand, paying bills and meticulously recording each check in a ledger for her accountant. The business was showing a profit, and by the end of the season she hoped to have enough saved to begin the remodeling projects she had in mind.

The ringing of her phone jarred the silence. She snatched it up on the second ring. "Yes?"

"I see by your lights that you're still up."

"Blair." She let out a long slow breath. "I thought you'd be asleep by now. Where are you?"

"Downstairs. Just below your balcony."

"Down...? Why didn't you just knock? Why are you calling my phone at a time like this?"

"I didn't want to frighten you. I figured this

would give you advance warning that I'm on my way up.''

She stared at the neat stack of bills. ''Go home. I don't want any visitors.''

''I made coffee.''

She stepped out onto the balcony and stared down through the mist swirling in off the lake to see him holding up a coffeepot. Even from this distance she thought she could smell the wonderful aroma of freshly ground beans.

''Hazelnut.'' His voice, rich and deep, floated up in the night air.

She let out a breath before calling out, ''Come around to the back door.''

By the time she'd descended the stairs, he was leaning against the doorway, wearing a silly grin.

''Think you're clever, don't you?'' She stood aside to allow him to precede her up the stairs to her apartment. ''Tempting me with coffee.''

As he brushed past her, he paused and breathed her in. ''Speaking of tempting... Bubble bath?''

She tried to ignore the little curl of pleasure along her spine. ''Yeah.''

''You smell like sin. Nobody should be allowed to smell that good.'' He sauntered past her and up the stairs, where he proceeded to retrieve two cups from her kitchen cupboard before filling them. He handed her one, and she took a moment to breathe in the wonderful aroma before lifting it to her lips.

She was aware of the look of pure male appreciation in his eyes as he studied the flow of the silk kimono over the curves and planes of her body. Though she cursed the fact that she hadn't pulled on a pair of old sweats, she would never give him the satisfaction of knowing she was uncomfortable under his scrutiny.

He ran a finger down her arm and felt the way she trembled slightly. "If I'd known this was how you look when you're lounging around, I'd have been here an hour ago."

"This old thing?" She flicked a glance down at herself before looking over at him. "If I'd known I was going to have company, I'd have put on something really sexy."

"Any sexier and I'd probably lose the last thread of my sanity."

"Really?" She gave a quick little cat smile. "That might be...interesting to watch."

His eyes narrowed. "Careful. This sounds suspiciously like flirting."

She chuckled, low in her throat. "Maybe it is."

"Courtney Brennan, man hater? What happens if I turn the tables and try my hand at seduction?"

"I have my reputation to uphold." She lifted

the cup to her mouth. "It takes two to play that game."

Before she could drink he caught her hand, stilling its movement. "I think you're lying. I think you're interested in joining in the game."

She looked at his hand, then up into his eyes. "Sorry. As I told you on the boat…"

Before she could finish, he took the cup from her hand and set it beside his on a side table.

"Blair, I…"

"Shh." His hands closed over her upper arms, and he dragged her close. Before she could offer any resistance he lowered his mouth to hers for a long, slow kiss that had the room spinning.

He took such care with her lips. As though they were the first he'd ever tasted. As though she were rich red wine, and he intended to drink his fill. The mere act had the desired effect of leaving her weak.

She was vaguely aware of her hands clutching his waist. Of her heartbeat speeding up until it throbbed at her temples. Of a long, deep sigh that rose up from somewhere inside her chest.

He ran soft, butterfly kisses over her upturned face before returning once more to her lips, where he drank from them again and again, unable to get enough of her.

Though his own breath was none too steady, he managed at last to lift his head and hold her a little away. "You can open your eyes now, Courtney."

Her lids snapped open and she found herself reflected in his eyes. The look on his face spoke more than any words. He'd been as affected by this as she.

"See. Flirting can lead to all kinds of... interesting games." He handed her back her cup before taking his own and settling himself into a chair.

She chose the chair at her desk across the room to put some distance between them. "Why aren't you asleep? The police have been gone for hours."

"Why aren't you?"

She shrugged. "Too keyed up."

"Yeah." He stared down into his cup. "I feel really bad about this, Courtney. I'm responsible for disrupting a lot of lives."

"I told you before, Blair. You didn't ask for this."

"Maybe not. But I certainly caused it."

"People have choices." She avoided his eyes, thinking about some of the disastrous choices she'd made, and the price she'd paid. "Nobody put a gun to their heads and told them to break into someone else's house. There are just some selfish, self-absorbed people in this world who don't give a single thought to what their careless, hurtful actions might do to someone else.''

''So much temper.'' He picked up the coffeepot and topped off her cup and then his own.

Courtney flushed. ''Sorry. I didn't mean to climb up on my soapbox.''

''Don't apologize. It's just that you're usually so controlled. I'd hate to have all that righteous anger directed toward me.''

His remark had the desired effect, and she dissolved into laughter. ''You don't ever want to see me use my left hook. I learned it from an amateur boxer at summer camp when I was twelve, and it's served me very well ever since.''

''I'll take your word for it.'' He nodded toward the neat stack of envelopes. ''Doing your books?''

''Yeah. I thought I'd put the time to good use.'' She glanced at the clock. ''I figured I might even get in a sail before I have to open the shop.''

''Then I'll leave you to it.'' He drained his cup before getting to his feet. ''I've got to be at the site earlier than usual this morning, since I'm meeting with the contractor.''

When she started to get up, he lifted a hand. "You don't have to see me out. I know the way."

"All right. I'll just sit here and enjoy the last of your excellent coffee."

"I'm glad you approve." As he started toward the stairs he paused and turned back. "Look, maybe I'm out of line, but I have to ask you something."

"Ask me what?"

"We've been concentrating on my aunt and who might want something of hers. But what if these break-ins were directed at you?" Seeing the way her hand bobbled the cup of coffee, he studied her in that cool, steady, under-the-microscope manner she'd come to recognize. "Made any enemies lately?"

"Of course not." But even to her own ears the words lacked conviction.

He shrugged. "Okay. Just checking. After all, you've lived in this town a lot longer than I have. I guess you'd know if there was someone out to get you."

"Of course I would."

She sat perfectly still as his footsteps echoed down the stairs. Hearing the door close, she got to her feet and watched from the balcony as he crossed the lawn that separated his place from hers.

Her coffee was forgotten, as was her plan for an early-morning sail. She headed toward her bedroom and dressed hurriedly before snatching up her car keys.

At The Willows, Courtney was relieved to find her grandfather puttering about in his garden. It would be easier to talk to him here, away from her grandmother and their housekeeper.

"'Morning, Poppie."

He looked up, and the pleasure in his eyes wrapped itself around her heart and tugged. "Courtney. What a nice surprise. Can you stay for breakfast?"

"I don't think so, Poppie."

"Trudy's making sourdough toast and crisp bacon. And I'm bringing in these tomatoes from the garden to go with it." He showed her the perfect tomatoes he'd already placed in a basket.

"Poppie, I need to talk to you." She took in a breath. "About Pietro."

The old man's tone softened. "You're wondering whether he could be behind these break-ins at Blair's place."

"Yes. I don't know why I never thought of it before. But it's become such a habit to never permit myself to think of him. Of that time. But Blair...asked me if I had any enemies, and that made me realize that I need to find out if Pietro could be behind this.''

''He isn't.'' Her grandfather took her hands in his. Cold, he realized. In the middle of summer, they were cold as ice. He mechanically began rubbing them between his big old leathery palms. ''I wondered when you'd get around to thinking of him. As soon as I was aware of what was happening here, I made a phone call and learned that Pietro is still in jail in Milan. He has another six months to serve.''

''Could he have contacted someone else to do this, to get even with me for prosecuting him?''

''He could. But I see no reason why he would. I think, from what his jailors told me, that he's as eager to put this behind him as you are, Courtney. They're calling him a reformed man and a model prisoner.''

She let out a long, slow breath. ''As long as you're satisfied that he isn't part of this, I am too, Poppie.'' And then another thought struck, and her eyes went wide. ''I lied to Blair. When he asked me if I knew of any enemies, I told him no.''

The old man drew her into the circle of his arms. "A little white lie, my darling. It's done sometimes, among friends, to save face. I'm sure you'll find a way to make it up to him, or possibly a time to come clean with the truth."

Against his chest she muttered, "Oh, Poppie, why does everything seem so much better when I'm with you?"

"Because I'm that rare and wonderful bird known as a grandfather." He held her away a little. "Now that we've solved the major problems of the world, why don't you come inside and join your grandmother and me for breakfast?"

"I wouldn't miss it for the world." She picked up the basket of tomatoes. "Especially if I get to pick which one of these I want with my sourdough toast."

"The choice is yours." He pressed a kiss to her cheek.

"I don't have a very good record in the choices department."

He dropped an arm around her shoulders. "That's how we learn, sweetheart. If all we ever made was right choices, how would we know how to survive the wrong ones?"

She wrapped an arm around his waist and moved along by his side, feeling such a glow of tenderness. This was why she loved him so. He had a way of turning the most negative event into a positive.

She had a feeling this was going to be a special day. Especially since it was beginning with her two favorite people in the whole world.

Chapter 11

Tourist season was in full swing. Crowds of people clogged the sidewalks, licking ice-cream cones and nibbling the town's famous fudge. Teens in their teeny-tiny shorts and tanks flirted shamelessly with boys in baggy cargos and muscle shirts. Women in flowing skirts and colorful wide-brimmed hats stopped at every store, sighing over hand-painted silk sweaters, coveting the one-of-a-kind ceramics and novelties. The men, walking several paces behind, paused to admire the latest fishing gear in the window of the Good Sportsman, or sat gratefully on the stone benches that

Courtney had cleverly spaced around the outer perimeter of Treasures.

In the past year better than half of all the sales of those benches had been made by long-suffering husbands, patiently sitting there while their wives shopped. Courtney made a mental note to order half a dozen more.

While Kendra was busy assisting several customers, Courtney glanced out the window at the workmen busy installing an alarm system at Blair's cottage. They'd already completed alarming her apartment, and had installed trouble lights around the building, guaranteed to go on whenever anyone got too close after dark.

It made her sad to realize how much the little town of Devil's Cove had grown into a big city. Just a few years ago it would have been unthinkable for anyone in town to lock a door or worry about vandals.

Still, it had to be done. She'd alarmed her shop as soon as she'd moved in and opened Treasures. Now it was a natural progression to do the same for her home. She and Blair couldn't go on worrying about these troublesome break-ins.

She and Blair. When had she begun to think of them as a team? It went against everything she'd worked so hard to build here. After Pietro, she'd been determined to make it alone. Both in business and in her personal life. It was true that a part of her was flattered by Blair's attentions. It would be so easy to give in to what he offered. Wasn't that what they both wanted? But when his job here was over and he went back to Greece or wherever his next job called him, what then? She knew only too well the price to be paid for a casual affair. One mistake may be acceptable. As Poppie had said, she'd learned from it. But twice? Shame on her.

"I've been in here three times in the past week." The woman in the designer jeans and denim shirt picked up a stunning glass sculpture and set it on the counter. "I've debated. I've argued. And every time I've talked myself out of this. But now I have to surrender. I simply must have this."

Courtney accepted the woman's credit card. "It's one of my favorite pieces."

"Mine, too." The woman sighed. "I have just the spot for this back home. I know if I don't buy it, I'll hate myself forever."

"We can't have that," Courtney said with a smile. "Will you take it with you, or have it shipped?"

"I'll take it with me. I want to admire it for the

next couple of days before we head home to Chicago.''

Courtney waited while the credit was approved, then began carefully swathing the sculpture in bubble wrap.

"Oh, I'm so glad nobody bought it before I could make up my mind."

Courtney handed over the heavy, handled bag. "I think that means you were meant to have it."

"I agree." The woman started toward the door and handed it to her husband before turning back. "By the way, I just love your shop."

"Thank you. You can't imagine how much I love hearing that."

Courtney was still smiling as she hurried over to assist yet another shopper. That piece had been one of the priciest in her store. The day was already showing a very good profit.

"Courtney."

She turned from the cash register to see the police chief standing at the counter. "Chief Thompson. Have you learned something?"

He peered out the window, where Kendra walked among the garden art, assisting customers. "Your little clerk and her boyfriend were spotted in a boat the night you scared off the vandals at Colby's cottage.''

Courtney felt a quick hitch around her heart. ''There's no law against being in a boat at night.''

''Pretty late for a couple of teens to be out. And it was just around the cove from here. They could have easily anchored it there, vandalized the cottage and disappeared without a trace.''

''For what reason, Boyd?''

He shook his head. ''That's the million-dollar question. Do they have a grudge against you or Colby?''

Courtney shook her head. ''Despite the strange hair and clothes, Kendra's a sweet girl. She's never missed a day of work since she started, right after graduation. I trust her with my shop and my cash register. I just can't believe she or her boyfriend would do anything like this.''

The police chief leaned close, keeping his voice soft. ''I just thought you ought to know. Right now, it doesn't seem wise to trust anybody.''

She nodded. ''All right. Thanks for the warning, Boyd.''

When he was gone, Courtney stood a moment watching Kendra charm a couple into buying an expensive garden statue of a little Dutch boy and girl. As she led them into the shop, she winked at Courtney.

What would have been a delightful moment between them just minutes ago, now seemed sly and contrived, as Courtney found herself wondering if this sweet young girl could be hiding a darker side.

After turning the sign on her door, Courtney hurried up the stairs to change into a bikini. There were still several hours of evening sunlight left, and she intended to savor every minute. She and Kendra had been on their feet without a break for most of the day.

Kendra.

Courtney shoved aside her worries as she slathered a couple of slices of bread with peanut butter, tucked them into a plastic bag and snagged a bottle of water from the refrigerator. After tossing them into her sea bag, she added a beach towel and a warm, hooded cover-up for the ride back after dark.

Sea bag in hand, she dashed downstairs and across the backyard toward her sailboat, anchored just beyond Blair's dock.

As she waded into the water, she heard the sound of footsteps on the dock and looked over to see Blair keeping stride with her. He was wearing bathing trunks and carrying a wicker hamper.

"Where are you going?"

He grinned. "Wherever the wind takes us, I guess."

"Us?" She lifted her sunglasses to peer at him. "I don't recall inviting you along."

"Of course you did. You told me I could come along anytime." Mimicking her, he lifted his sunglasses. "I figure this is as good a time as any."

She glanced suspiciously toward the hamper. "What's in there?"

"Brie. A loaf of crusty bread fresh from the Devil's Cove Bakery. Cold chicken. And a bottle of really expensive champagne."

Her smile was quick and sassy. "You just won a chance to be my navigator. Welcome aboard, sailor."

With a laugh he jumped off the dock and followed her through the shallows to the boat.

After climbing aboard and stowing their gear, they set about their routine with few words needed between them. While Blair hauled anchor, Courtney unfurled the sails. She manned the tiller while he handled the rigging. In no time they were skimming across the waves under a cloudless sky.

He watched the way the wind took her hair,

sending it streaming out behind her. She lifted her face to the sun and he could see the look of pure pleasure in her eyes.

"Did you get many chances to sail in Italy?"

"No." The smile was gone, erased instantly, and he wondered about it, regretting the fact that it had been his careless question that caused it.

He kept his tone conversational. "I did some sailing in Greece. The islands are like tiny jewels."

"So I've heard." She forced herself to relax. "I think I'd like to sail there someday."

"I'd love to show them to you." He secured the ropes and crossed the deck to stand beside her. "When I sailed past Santorini, I could see wild donkeys up in the hills. The houses look like they're about to tumble into the sea. But they cling, like the tough little plants that grow between the cracks in the rocks. Like the tough people who have endured there for centuries."

"Sounds like poetry. You loved it, didn't you?"

He nodded.

"Will you go back?" She wasn't even aware that she was holding her breath.

"I think about it. I'm sure I'll go back for a

visit now and then. But I think I'm ready to settle down and make my home in the States now."

His statement surprised her. "Won't you find it dull, after living in Greece?"

He shrugged. "Do you?"

She looked away. "It's different for me."

"In what way?"

She kept her eyes averted. "My memories of Italy aren't entirely happy. And when I returned, I knew I was coming home."

"Yeah." He jammed his hands in his pockets to keep from touching her. It was all he'd been thinking about. Drawing her close. Feeling the press of her body to his. "Home's a great place to be when you're leaving unhappy memories behind."

She looked over. "It wasn't all unhappy. It just...ended badly."

Because he hated the look in her eyes he quickly changed the subject. "What's that island over there?"

"The locals call it Turtle Island, because it's shaped like a turtle. It's just a little patch of sand and vegetation in the middle of the lake."

"Can we get close enough to anchor and have dinner?"

"Oh, sure." She turned the tiller and they

headed toward the island. "There's a nice sandy beach for swimming, and no dangerous rocks or shallows that I know of."

When they were close enough to drop anchor, they clamored over the side of the boat and waded to shore. Once there, Courtney opened her sea bag and spread the beach towel in the shade of a weathered rock.

Blair popped the cork on the champagne and filled two foaming flutes before handing one to her. "Here's to perfect summer nights."

She touched her glass to his.

Before she could sip he added, "And to all the things we can find to amuse ourselves on this deserted island."

She met his eyes. "Dream on, Colby."

He merely smiled. "You can't blame a guy for his fantasies."

"Just so he knows the difference between fantasy and reality."

"Courtney, darling, I'd love to show you how to turn one into the other."

"I'm not interested. And I'm not your darling." She glanced down at the hamper. "Are you going to share that brie?"

He knelt on the beach towel and reached for a

knife. Minutes later they were enjoying crusty bread spread with cheese.

"Oh." Courtney sighed. "This is so much better than my peanut butter sandwiches."

"That was going to be your dinner?"

"Uh-huh."

"Then I know you're going to love this." He unwrapped the foil covering and offered her a piece of chicken.

She leaned her back against the sun-warmed rock and ate in silence. He settled himself beside her and did the same. When her glass was empty, he picked up the bottle and filled it, before topping off his own.

She sipped, watching the sea birds that dipped and wheeled overhead, hoping to snatch a few crumbs. "You realize they want their share."

He nodded. "They'll have to be patient." He stretched out his long legs, crossing them at the ankle. "A guy could get used to living like this. I can see why you decided to stay."

"It does cast a spell, doesn't it?" She was smiling as she looked over at him.

"So do you, Courtney." The look in his eyes had her heart slamming against her ribs. "This has to be some kind of spell. Why else would I risk insult, rejection and flat-out refusal so many times, and keep coming back for more?''

He didn't touch her. Maybe that was what held her attention. That, and the fact that his voice, though little more than a whisper, was so fierce.

He curled his fingers into his palms, all the while staring into her eyes. ''I think I've figured you out. Some guy battered your heart, and you're never going to let anyone get close enough to allow it to happen again. Fair enough, I suppose. Of course, there's a good chance that the right guy might come along, and after a while give up, and you'll never even know what you lost. Still, it's your heart. You've got the right to protect it.''

Her tone was sarcastic as she scrambled to her feet. ''I'm glad you've got it all figured out.''

''That's right.'' He followed her lead and stood. His voice lowered. ''What I haven't figured out is me. Why the hell am I still here, and still trying, when you've made it clear you're not interested?''

Her head came up. ''Blair…''

He cut her off. ''Don't tell me you're a witch, because I don't believe in them.''

She'd wanted, desperately, to keep things light. But she was afraid it was all getting out of hand. ''What do you believe in?''

He closed his hands over the tops of her arms.

"Things I can see, touch, smell." Without thinking he dragged her close and pressed his face to her hair, breathing her in. "You're real, Courtney. Maybe the first real woman I've ever known."

She wasn't sure what touched her more. The words he spoke or the way he spoke them. As though torn from the depths of his soul.

She could feel the way he was fighting for control. It excited her even as it frightened her.

She lifted her face to his. "Kiss me."

Instead of doing as she'd asked, he frowned and, without warning, released her and turned away.

"What's wrong?" Without thinking she laid a hand on his bare back and felt him flinch.

His voice was a warning growl. "Unless you're ready to spend the next couple of hours on this island fulfilling my fantasies, don't do that again. You might want to think about packing up the hamper. Or maybe going for a swim. I know that's what I'm going to do."

Without another word he strode past her and into the water. She stood on shore, watching as he sank beneath the waves. Moments later he surfaced and began, with powerful strokes, to swim past the boat and out to the deeper water.

When there was enough distance between them,

she followed suit and stepped into the water. After all, this was what she'd planned in the first place. A pleasant sail, a quick supper and a moonlight swim. Alone. And now she had her wish.

Then why was she feeling so miserable?

Because, a nagging little voice taunted, she'd been more aroused by his touch than she cared to admit. She had a pretty good idea that his fantasies were much more fulfilling than hers.

She rolled to her back and began to float, closing her eyes to the night sky. She didn't want to see that big fat moon. Didn't want to watch the twinkle of stars in the heavens. They taunted her with thoughts of what might have been.

"Having fun yet?"

Blair's voice, so close, had her jumping. "Don't sneak up on me like that."

"I wasn't sneaking. Just swimming. And as far as I can see, the lake belongs to everybody. Or do you have a private claim on this spot?"

She arched a brow. "As a matter of fact, I do. Maybe you haven't heard that the Brennan family has owned this particular strip of Lake Michigan for generations."

He grinned. "Good try. But you're a lousy liar, Brennan."

"Says you."

"Says your eyes. They give you away every time."

"Prove it."

"All right." He closed a hand around her upper arm and drew her close, all the while treading water.

When Courtney tried to touch bottom, she realized she was too short. There was nothing to do but allow him to prove or disprove his statement.

He grinned. "If you don't mind, I'll need to stare deeply into your eyes for this."

She stared back without blinking.

"It's simple, really. Tell me you don't want to kiss me, Courtney."

She tossed her head. "I don't want to kiss you."

"Caught you lying."

"How would you know that?"

"Because…" He let go of her and framed her face with his hands.

Her reaction was automatic. Without a firm foundation beneath her feet, she was forced to reach for his waist and cling.

His voice was warm with laughter. "Why, Miss Brennan. I do believe you can't keep your hands off me."

"Go to—"

His mouth closed over hers, cutting off whatever she'd been about to say. The kiss was long and slow and deliberate, as though he had all the time in the world to taste her sweetness. He was aware of her soft little sigh and the way her hands tightened at his waist.

It occurred to Courtney that no man had ever made her feel this completely, thoroughly kissed. As though he'd somehow lost himself in her and couldn't find his way out. It was the most erotic feeling. Especially since she'd become lost in him, as well.

When at last he lifted his head, she shivered from the loss of his mouth on hers.

She was dismayed to see him step back. "Where are you going?"

"Back to shore. I need some space. And so do you."

What upset her even more than his words was the angry, almost bleak look in his eyes in that instant before he turned away.

Not at all like a man who'd just been indulging in something pleasurable.

Chapter 12

Courtney walked through the shallows. On shore Blair was busy toweling himself.

"Nice kiss, Colby. But it didn't prove a thing." She picked up her beach towel and began to dry herself off.

"It proved enough."

"That I'm not strong enough to fight you?"

"Oh, baby, that was as far from a fight as it could be. You were as lost in that kiss as I was."

There was no denying the truth, as much as it rankled. "Maybe. But I don't consider that the ultimate test."

"And that would be…?"

"Dry land. You know. A level playing field."

"Playing field? You're still into playing games?" When he turned, his eyes were narrowed on her. "You might want to step back a few paces and give me some space."

"And if I don't?"

Something flared in his eyes. Something dark and dangerous that had her pulse racing. "In case you haven't figured it out yet, the time for harmless flirting is over, Courtney. I'm on a thin tether here."

"Maybe you're not the only one." She saw his eyes widen as the meaning of her words dawned.

Still he didn't touch her. Instead he merely shook his head. "You've already made it plain that you're not interested in a casual relationship. And if that isn't a big enough barrier, think about all those regrets you'll have to deal with later. I'm assuming it's regret that's been hanging like a millstone around that pretty neck of yours."

"Yeah." The word came out on a sigh. "I guess I have been playing the blame game too long. After a while, it gets to be a habit. But tell me something. Why are you going to all this trouble to talk me out of…my feelings?"

"Oh? You're having feelings? Just what are they?"

"It would be a lot easier to talk about this if you'd use a gentler tone. And maybe…hold me, Blair."

He draped the towel around his neck and kept his hands firmly clenched to either end of it. "Sorry. I don't think that's a good idea."

Seeing that he wasn't about to budge, she reached up to close a hand over his. "Don't be mad. It's just that I'm not sure what I'm feeling anymore."

"Not good enough." Despite the flare of heat from her touch, he took a step back. "I know you well enough by now to know that you're a woman with a mind of your own. If you're waiting for the big seduction, so you can claim to be swept off your feet and out of your mind, find another guy."

"You're not interested in seducing me?" She tried to laugh, though it came out in a sound that was more like a sigh. "Or are you suggesting that you'd rather I seduce you?"

He was looking at her with a bemused expression. "That might prove interesting."

"You don't think I can?"

"In a heartbeat. I'm easy. I'm just wondering

how you'll deal with all that crushing guilt in the morning.''

"Let me worry about my guilt.''

His grin was quick and deadly. "Gladly.'' He seemed to brace himself, feet planted squarely in the sand, hands on his hips. "You can start the seduction anytime you're ready. If you think you're up for it.''

Instead of facing him she walked around him once, twice.

"Looking for my weakness? Or are we into wrestling now? Thinking of taking me two out of three falls?''

Instead of answering him she merely walked around him a third time. This time she paused and touched a hand to the small of his back. Just the lightest touch, but she felt his quivering response and it made her smile.

"I believe I've just found your weakness.''

"Not fair.'' He took a step back, laughing. "I'm ticklish there.''

"And here?'' When he turned to face her she placed a hand on his flat stomach, then moved it upward, across his chest. "Hmm. You seem to have a lot of those ticklish spots.''

He closed a hand over hers to keep it from wandering farther. ''You're playing a dangerous game, you know.''

''Maybe I like dangerous games.'' She stood on tiptoe to brush a kiss over his mouth, and heard his quick intake of breath. ''And dangerous men.''

It was the softest of kisses. A mere butterfly brush of mouth to mouth, but the feelings that pulsed between them rocked them back on their heels.

His hands closed over her upper arms. Though his eyes were narrowed on her, his head was spinning. The slightest touch of her had his nerves quivering. That simple kiss had shattered all his defenses. Why did she have to smell so clean and fresh, like the lake? Why did her wet hair have to bear the unmistakable fragrance of a summer garden? He wanted to bury his face there. To lose himself in her. To taste her. All of her. Now. Before he went mad from the wanting.

If it were that simple, he would take her here and now, and to hell with tomorrow. Instead, for her sake, he struggled to hold his own feelings in check. ''Okay. You've proved your point. You're good at seduction.''

She gave him a little smile. ''I haven't even begun.''

"It doesn't matter." He held up his hands. "I told you I'm easy. I surrender."

"What if I don't accept surrender?"

He touched a hand to the narrow strap of her bikini. "Then be warned. If we take this to the next step, you'd better be prepared for those fantasies I told you about."

"Maybe I'm looking forward to them."

"You think so?" He watched her eyes as he drew the strap across her shoulder and down her arm. "I remember the night I arrived in Devil's Cove and you came dashing out of your place ready to attack like a little pit bull."

"I thought you were an intruder."

He smiled. "And so I was. But I remember thinking that if I hadn't been driving for all those hours, and so tired I was nearly blind, it might have been fun to go a couple of rounds with you." His tone lowered seductively. "I'm not tired tonight, Courtney. I have all this restless energy building up inside. And what I want is an even match with that same tough little woman who was determined to defend a stranger's cottage, no matter what the cost. Of course—" he reached for the other strap and drew it down her arm "—I'll also want you out of that bikini so I can touch and taste and feast on you until I've had my fill. No barriers between us tonight, I promise you.''

Maybe he'd expected his words to be a dash of cold water, in case there were any lingering doubts. At the least, he'd expected to see shock in her eyes. Or censure. Instead, his words seemed to have the opposite effect.

For a moment Courtney said nothing as she stared into his eyes. The moment he'd touched her, her throat felt so parched she wondered if she could speak a single word. It wasn't necessary.

The look in her eyes had the blood pumping hot through his veins.

His tone was rough. ''No more games. No more tests. I want you to be sure.''

''I am.'' She wondered if her voice sounded as tremulous to him as it did to her.

''Just so you know. If you're having second thoughts, you'd better say so now. Loud and clear. Because otherwise—'' he drew her fractionally closer, all the while staring into her eyes ''—I'll make the decision for both of us.''

''I make my own decisions.'' Though the words nearly strangled her, she managed to say them before his mouth crushed hers.

His arms closed around her, cupping her hips and dragging her roughly against him. And all the while his mouth plundered hers until he seemed to steal the very breath from her lungs.

At first all she could do was hold on as he took her on a dizzying ride. When at last his mouth left hers, she sucked in great gulps of air and struggled for control, only to lose it when he began nibbling hot, wet kisses along the sensitive column of her throat. A sound more animal than human escaped her lips as she arched her neck, giving him easier access. He lingered there, pressing light, feathery kisses to the hollow of her neck and shoulder, then lower, until he encountered her bikini top.

''No barriers. Not tonight.'' In one swift motion he unsnapped it and tossed it aside, freeing her breasts.

For the space of a heartbeat he merely studied her in the spill of moonlight. ''How can you be so beautiful? So perfect.''

He kissed her again, while his hands moved over her with a sort of reverence that had her breath backing up in her lungs.

''You're beautiful, too.'' She needed to have her hands on him. She loved the feel of all that lean flesh and corded muscle beneath her fingertips.

Now that she was free to touch him, she couldn't seem to get enough. It gave her such pleasure to hear his quick moan when she ran hot, wet kisses across his chest.

Annoyed with even the slightest barrier between them, he tugged aside her bikini bottom and shed his trunks before gathering her so close she could feel the pounding of his heartbeat inside her own chest.

His kisses were more urgent, as his hands, those wonderful hands, continued driving her closer and closer to the edge of insanity.

She wondered that she was still able to stand. Her body felt so gloriously alive, her bones as fluid as quicksilver. She draped herself around him, wanting, needing, to feel him in every part of her. With her arms wrapped around his neck she returned his kisses with a fervor that had him reeling.

He took her hands, and they dropped to their knees on the beach towels.

He framed her face, staring into those big luminous eyes, and wondered at the feelings flowing through him for this woman. In the moonlight she looked like a golden, glorious mermaid. All that long silky hair and skin kissed by the sun. But this was a flesh-and-blood woman, about to give him the most precious of all gifts.

He had to shake off the desire to take her, hard

and fast. It was what he wanted, what they both wanted, to end this terrible, driving need that had them trembling. But she needed more. So much more. If he was right, if she'd been hurt in the past, it was his only chance to get it right. And so he forced himself to slow down. To soothe. To savor. To give, as well as take.

He stretched out and drew her down beside him, all the while kissing her, stroking her back, her arm, her side, until he could feel her begin to relax in his embrace.

When he ran soft, nibbling kisses down her throat to her shoulder, she arched her neck and wondered that she wasn't purring like a kitten. Or was she? The thought had her smiling. But when he brought his mouth lower to close over her nipple, she let out a gasp of surprise that quickly became a sigh of pleasure. And then his fingers found her, hot and wet, and without warning he drove her to the first glorious peak.

She was wonderful to watch. The way those big eyes went wide with shock before her body arched, taut as a bow, and then that dazed, stunned expression as she reached the crest.

He gave her no time to recover before he closed his mouth over hers and took her up and over

again, making her body hum with needs she'd
never even known she possessed.

For Courtney the need to be in control was vital
to her very survival. Now, realizing how quickly
it had all gotten out of hand, she felt a moment
of pure panic. But then, with his mouth on hers,
and those wonderful hands moving over her, she
realized that she hadn't lost control. She'd given
it. Freely. And would gladly do it again, if only
he would never stop.

"Blair." She struggled to see him through the
blaze of passion that clouded her vision. But all
she could see were his eyes, staring into hers with
that fierce expression that grabbed her by the
throat and had her heart racing. There was a darkness here, a danger, that excited her.

"Hold on, baby."

They came together in a fierce kiss that was all
fire and flash and blinding, desperate passion.
Bodies wet and slick, lungs straining, they took
each other on a wild ride. When at last he entered
her she let out a cry. Half-crazed with desire she
wrapped herself around him, moving with him,
climbing with him, matching her strength to his.

He framed her face with his hands, determined
to watch her eyes. "Courtney."

Her name, torn from his lips, had her eyes going wide. Through a burning mist of passion she struggled to focus on him.

"Blair," she whispered his name like a prayer.

And then they knew only this incredible strength as they began to climb. Their breathing was labored as they reached the very pinnacle of a high, sheer mountain peak. For just an instant they seemed to hover there. And then, gazes still locked, they stepped off the edge into space.

And soared.

Chapter 13

Blair's voice sounded strangled. "That was…"

"…incredible." She couldn't help finishing his thought.

"Mmm." With his face still resting in the hollow of her throat, he felt too dazed to move.

And so they lay in a tangle of arms and legs, amid the twisted towels, feeling the breeze off the water begin to cool their overheated flesh.

He managed to lift his face enough to stare into her eyes. "Sorry I was so rough."

"You weren't. You were…sweet." She touched a fingertip to his cheek, then dropped her hand to her side, as if the gesture had been too great an effort.

"You're amazing, Courtney." He levered himself on one elbow to trace a finger along the curve of her cheek. "All that passion hidden inside one very cool package."

"Sometimes it doesn't pay to advertise."

That had him chuckling. He sobered. "I'm feeling a little guilty right now."

Her eyes snapped open. "I thought I owned the franchise on guilt."

He frowned. "I had this all planned, you know."

"What?"

"This evening. I was watching to see when you closed up shop. Saw your lights on upstairs and guessed you were getting ready to sail. The minute you stepped out your door I was ready to fall into step beside you and talk my way onboard."

"And this?"

He nodded. "Part of the plan. But then I decided I had no right, and went for a cold swim instead."

"A man with a conscience."

He shrugged. "Something like that. I was feeling like a louse for wanting to seduce you."

"That experiment in the lake?"

He looked sheepish. "Hey, my heart was in the right place. I was trying to do the right thing, but I'm a guy. I just had to give it one more try."

Courtney couldn't help laughing. "Well, I'm glad you didn't give up on me."

"Then you're not sorry about this?"

"Sorry?" She wrapped her arms around his neck and drew him down for a long, lazy kiss. "Mr. Colby, right now I'm feeling so good, I just might offer you a two-for-one deal. That is, if you think you're up for another."

He pulled back to stare into her eyes, before pressing his mouth to her throat with a growl of laughter that had her shivering.

"Up for it? Oh, lady, how can any red-blooded male pass up an offer like that?"

The darkness was punctuated with their laughter, which gradually turned into sighs and whispered words of endearment, as they took each other on a slow journey of discovery.

Blair and Courtney lay comfortably huddled together in their towels and hooded cover-ups, feeling pleasantly sated. Sparks from their campfire they'd set using driftwood they found along the shore sent bright flashes of light dancing in the darkness.

"I had a visit today from Chief Thompson."

Though Courtney spoke casually enough, Blair felt the hum of tension at her words. "Did he have some news?"

"Only that Kendra and Eddie were spotted in a boat just around the cove from our place right after we scared off the vandal the other night."

"Does he think they're involved?"

She shrugged. "Boyd thinks everyone is guilty until proven innocent. That's his job."

"What do you think?"

Again that shrug. "She's worked for me all summer. I like her. And I can't think of a single reason why she would want to break into my place or yours."

"How about her boyfriend?"

"I don't know him well, but Kendra really likes him."

"Maybe he's leading her down a garden path."

"Of crime?" She sighed. "I don't know what to think, Blair. I hate the thought that I'm beginning to mistrust my own employee."

He drew her close and kissed her gently. "And I hate that you have to spend even one minute worrying about this." He quickly changed the subject. "I've decided to rename this place. I think—" he played with a strand of her hair, loving the feel of it between his fingers "—instead of Turtle Island, we ought to call it Fantasy Island."

"Hmm." She smiled up at him. "You do have some rather...interesting fantasies. Thanks for sharing."

His grin was quick and dangerous. "Happy to oblige, ma'am. Yours aren't bad, either."

"I'm glad you approve." She took a bite of brie spread on thick, crusty bread, and handed him the other half. They'd already finished the last of the chicken and champagne. "Looks like the only thing left is some peanut butter sandwiches and a bottle of water."

"Then I think it's time to head home."

Courtney wondered if she had the energy to rouse herself. She would gladly spend the night here, lying in Blair's arms, far away from the suspicion and mistrust that seemed to have settled like a pall over their lives. Still, she supposed it was a good thing one of them was being practical.

As she started to sit up, Blair drew her close for a long, slow kiss. When at last they came up for air, he muttered thickly, "Are you in a hurry?"

"No. Why?"

There was that killer smile again, sending her

heart into overdrive. "I just figured we may as
well take advantage of the privacy here...and
those stars, and that moon."

Laughing, she fell into his arms and raised her
mouth for another of his drugging kisses. "You
just talked me into it."

"You're easy, Ms. Brennan."

"Almost as easy as you, Mr. Colby."

"Home, sweet home." Courtney planted her
feet and began hauling down the rigging while
Blair tossed the anchor over the side.

Within minutes they had the boat secured and
were trudging through the shallows, juggling her
sea bag and his hamper. When they reached the
door of his cottage, he set down the hamper and
caught her hand.

"Stay the night, Courtney."

She paused. "Why not come up to my place
instead?"

He shook his head. "This is closer."

"By a few steps."

He drew her close and brushed his mouth over
hers. "On a night like this, every step counts."

When they stepped apart she shivered. "Yeah.
I see what you mean."

"Besides, I'll start a fire, and while you're showering, I'll make you coffee."

"You really know how to tempt a girl, don't you?"

"You bet." He grinned. "I have no intention of playing fair."

She sighed. "All right. But I don't even have any clean clothes for the morning."

"Like you said, it's just a few steps away. I'll loan you my robe for the walk home."

"Gee. Thanks, sport." She was laughing as she followed him into his cottage.

He turned on a light and punched in the code for the new alarm system, then drew her back into his arms and kissed her until she could feel her head spinning.

She looked up at him. "Now what was that kiss all about?"

"That was just for me." He kissed the tip of her nose. "I'm glad you're spending the night, Court." He caught her hand. "Come on. I'll show you to the shower."

"I can find my own way."

"Yeah, but I thought you might like some help."

"What I'd like is that coffee you promised me."

"I can take a hint." He snapped on his bedroom light, rummaged in his closet until he'd located a terry robe, which he tossed on his bed, and left her alone.

When she stepped out of the shower minutes later she could smell coffee brewing. With a smile she pulled on Blair's robe and padded to the kitchen.

It was a jolt to see her in his robe, wet hair streaming down her back in a tangle of curls.

He handed her a steaming cup.

"A man of his word. I like that." She sipped, then gave a sigh of pleasure. "Oh, that's perfect coffee."

"I'm glad you approve." Up close, her face scrubbed free of makeup was so perfect he had to touch a finger to it.

She blinked. "What are you doing?"

"Touching you." He leaned close and brushed a kiss to her cheek. "Would you mind very much setting down that coffee?"

"Why?"

He took the cup from her hand and dragged her close. "Because I have to kiss you. Right this minute. And I'd rather not have either of us burned."

She opened her mouth to respond, but the moment his mouth found hers, all thought fled.

"I like you in my robe." He muttered the words thickly against her throat while his hands found the sash at her waist. "But I'll like you even more out of it."

And then there were no more words as they took each other on a wild, breathless ride.

"Mmm." Courtney sat up, shoving tangles from her eyes. Sometime during the night they'd made their way to Blair's bed. "Is that fresh coffee?"

Blair, wearing a pair of denims that rode low on his hips, set a tray on the bedside table and handed her a steaming cup. "I figured it was the least I could do after that brief interruption."

"Brief?" She glanced at the clock. "That was nearly three hours ago."

"Amazing how much we can accomplish in just three hours." He slathered strawberry jam on a scone and offered her a bite.

"Oh, that's heavenly."

He was watching the way the sheet barely covered her nakedness. "I was just thinking the same thing."

Courtney laughed, feeling completely unself-conscious. "You're insatiable."

"Now you know my secret." He picked up his own cup of coffee and settled himself beside her in the bed. "Know what I like about you?"

"What?" She studied him over the rim of her cup.

"Everything."

"That's understandable. I am, after all, perfect."

He grinned. "Did I say everything? I meant to say everything except that lack of self-esteem. Your inferiority complex is becoming a real problem."

They laughed easily together.

Blair leaned back, feeling more relaxed than he could ever recall. She was so easy to be with. If he could, he would hold back the dawn and let this perfect night spin on forever.

He linked her fingers with his and lifted them to his mouth. "I could get used to this."

He saw her quick frown. "I've said something wrong."

"No." She withdrew her hand and took a sip of coffee before setting aside her cup. "It's just that I've learned not to plan too far into the future."

"Milan."

The word hung between them until she sighed and nodded. "There was a man. Pietro. My business partner and my..." She shrugged. "He cheated in both areas of my life, and when it was over, and I was left with bad debts and a lot of unresolved anger, I felt foolish and angry...and used. Especially since I had to turn to my grandfather for legal advice."

"You're lucky you had someone to turn to."

She nodded. "I know. But I hated having to confess my stupidity."

"Knowing your grandfather, I doubt he'd call it stupid. There are takers in this world, Court. They feed off the good people." He caught her hand and lifted it again to his mouth. "And you're definitely one of the good ones."

"And how would you know that?"

"It's there in your eyes for anybody who bothers to look." He drew her close and pressed a kiss to her temple, her cheek, the corner of her mouth. Against her lips he whispered, "I'm grateful to Pietro. If he hadn't betrayed you, you'd have never left Milan. And then I would have never had the chance to meet you. Do you know that the first time I met you, I knew?"

"Knew what?"

"I knew—" he drew her fully into the kiss, breathing the words inside her mouth "—I had to taste your goodness, or die trying."

She felt such a welling of emotion as he poured himself into the kiss. And then she was lost. Lost in the most exquisite pleasure as he showered her with long, deep kisses that had fireworks exploding behind her closed lids, and touches that sent slivers of fire and ice coursing through her veins. She was helpless to do more than sigh and cling to him as he took her on the most incredible journey of love.

Chapter 14

Courtney awoke and lay a minute, trying to get her bearings. It all came back to her in a rush of feelings. The night she'd spent with Blair. The things they'd done. The private little stories about their past they'd shared. She'd told him about her family. Her father, the town doctor, and the pride she felt in the way her mother carried on after his death. The love she shared with her three sisters. The deep bond of affection they all enjoyed with their grandparents. Blair had proven to be a good listener. It was so easy to tell him anything. Everything.

But he'd shared little about his own family. There seemed to be areas of his life too painful to talk about. She understood that kind of pain and resolved to be patient. He would tell her in his own way, his own time.

She lay back, listening to the sound of water running in the shower. She breathed in the wonderful perfume of coffee perking in the kitchen. Outside the window, a chorus of birds had begun their morning symphony.

There was such a good feeling in this cottage. A feeling of homey comfort mixed with solid, hardworking virtues. Did these feelings have to do with Blair? Or had they been here all along, perhaps a legacy from his aunt? Whatever the source, it felt good to be here.

He stepped from the shower, wearing a towel draped low on his hips. "'Morning." He paused beside the bed and bent to brush a kiss over her lips. "You're looking awfully happy about something."

"I was thinking how much I like your cottage. There's a good feeling here."

He sat on the edge of the bed and took her hand. "You feel it, too?"

She nodded. "There's just something." She shrugged. "It makes me happy."

He was staring into her eyes with such intensity. "The first time I felt it, I couldn't understand. I was only eight. But each time I came back, it was here, as though waiting for me. This time I figured I was too old to feel it again, but it was still here, like an old friend, waiting all those years to greet me. Now I don't even question it. Each day, when I walk through that door, I sense that the feeling will be here. And it is."

"Oh, Blair. That's so wonderful."

He grinned. "Yeah. I've never told another soul about this. What is it about you that I can tell you things that would make other people question my sanity?"

"Maybe because I'm as crazy as you?"

He nodded. "That must be it." He kissed the tip of her nose and started out of the room.

"Where are you going?"

"Coffee." Minutes later he returned with two cups and handed one to her.

"You're spoiling me, you know." She sat up against the cushions and breathed in the fragrance of freshly ground beans before taking her first sip.

"Maybe I have good reason to."

When she lifted a brow he smiled. "I'm hoping to persuade you to come back after work tonight and give me a chance for a repeat performance."

"Ah." She ducked her head and took another sip.

When he began to dress she sat up and slipped into his robe.

He caught sight of her reflection in the mirror. "You thinking of making the dash to your place in that?"

She nodded. "Not too many people up and about at this hour. Those who are might think I was taking a swim."

"Uh-huh." He knotted his tie, then turned and dragged her close for a long, slow kiss. "I don't care what they think. Just so you promise you'll let me feed you as soon as you're through working for the day."

She returned the kiss. "You're making this way too hard for me to refuse."

Against her temple he whispered, "That's the plan."

She picked up her sea bag and stepped out into the morning mist. As she dashed across the yard and disappeared inside her apartment it occurred to her that she'd stopped fretting about the past, or worrying about the future. All that mattered was now, this day, and seeing Blair when the workday ended.

Was this some sort of magic? Or was it just

Blair? Or could it be that they were one and the same? Maybe the magic was inside Blair and it had somehow found a way to touch her, too. Whatever the answer, she wouldn't dwell on it. She would simply relax and go with her feelings.

"Good night, Kendra."

The young woman picked up her denim bag from a cupboard behind the counter and slung it over her shoulder. Instead of walking away, she paused. "I think you ought to know, Court. The police stopped Eddie and me the other night when we were out on his boat."

"Chief Thompson told me."

The girl blinked. "He did?"

"Yeah."

"You didn't say anything." She licked her lips. "We didn't do anything wrong, Court."

"I'm glad."

Kendra paused. "That's it? You're not going to fire me or anything?"

"You just said you didn't do anything wrong. Why would I fire you?"

The girl stared at the toe of her thrift-shop espadrilles. "I know a lot of people in town think Eddie and I are freaks."

Courtney laid a hand over hers. "Kendra, you

show up on time every day, you joke with my customers, and you give me a full day's work for your pay. I can't ask any more than that from you. How you dress, the color of your hair and what you and Eddie do after hours are none of my business.''

The girl's smile bloomed. ''You know something, Court? You're cool.'' She started out the door and called over her shoulder, '''Night, Courtney. See you tomorrow.''

''Yeah.'' Courtney locked the door behind her and flipped over the sign before heading up the stairs to her apartment.

Half an hour later, dressed in a summery, ankle-skimming white gown and matching sandals, she picked up a weekend bag and headed across the backyard to Blair's cottage.

Before she could knock, the door was thrust open and Blair hauled her into his arms, kissing her until she could feel her head spinning.

When at last they came up for air she managed a startled laugh. ''That was some greeting, Mr. Colby. You'd think we've been apart for years instead of mere hours.''

''Has it only been hours?'' He kissed her again, thoroughly, before taking her hand and leading her inside. "Sorry. But I missed you way too much."

"I missed you, too."

"Good. I'd hate to think I was alone in this madness."

"An apt description." She looked around and realized he'd set the table with fine china and crystal. "Something smells wonderful."

"I picked up dinner at the Harbor House. I thought about taking you there, but I couldn't stand the thought of having to share you with all those people in that big, elegant dining room." He popped the cork on a bottle of champagne and poured two frothy glasses. "So I talked the chef into making us something special that we could enjoy here instead."

"You must have some powers of persuasion. The Harbor House doesn't do takeout."

"So they told me." He handed her a glass. "But in the end I prevailed."

She laughed. "I have an idea you're used to getting your way."

"Sometimes. When it's really important." He touched his glass to hers. "Here's to us, Courtney."

"To us." She saw the way his eyes stayed

steady on hers, and felt his caress as surely as if he'd touched her.

Suddenly dinner didn't seem important. Nor did the champagne. She drank, but only to soothe the dryness in her throat. Then she set the glass aside and stepped closer to touch a hand to his cheek. "I could hardly concentrate today. All I could think about was you."

"Yeah." He set aside his glass and framed her face with his hands. "Would you mind letting dinner wait?"

Her smile wrapped itself around his heart. "I thought you'd never ask."

"Chef Henri's steak and lobster was perfect." Blair sat back on a wave of contentment and sipped his champagne.

"The chocolate-dipped strawberries weren't bad, either."

He nodded. "Henri suggested éclairs, but I thought they'd be too heavy."

"The strawberries were a good choice."

He eyed the overnight bag that lay forgotten just inside the door. "I hope that means that you're planning on staying the night."

"I am. And I didn't want to try another dash to my place in your robe. So I brought enough clothes for tomorrow's brunch at my grandparents'. I hope you'll come with me.''

''I wouldn't miss it.'' He reached across the table and caught her hand, rubbing his thumb across her wrist. ''I don't know what I did to deserve you, but I won't question the fates.''

She felt a quickening of her pulse and wondered at his ability to affect her so dramatically with nothing more than a simple touch.

She pushed away from the table. ''I'll help clear away the dishes.''

It took only a few minutes to load the dishwasher. When they'd finished, Blair nodded toward her bag. ''Want to unpack?''

''I may as well. I didn't bring much with me.'' She picked up the bag. ''Where should I put my things?''

He led the way to his bedroom and glanced around. ''The drawers in my aunt's old desk are empty. Why don't you use those?''

She nodded and set the bag on his bed before opening first the smaller drawer, where she settled her lingerie, then the deeper one, where she planned to stash her purse and shoes. She stared down with a puzzled frown.

Catching the look on her face, he paused. ''What's wrong?''

"Nothing. But I expected this drawer to be much deeper." She closed it, studied the depth, then opened it and pointed. "Look. From the outside, it appears to be much bigger than the other drawer. But when you open it, there's no more space than in the smaller one."

Blair studied the drawer for a moment, then reached inside and tapped it, before turning to her with a look of understanding.

"Well, I'll be... It has a false bottom."

"But why?"

He shook his head. "Let's find out."

Feeling around, he found a bit of frayed leather that appeared to be attached to the bottom of the drawer. When he gave it a hard, quick tug, the false bottom lifted up, revealing something beneath.

For long silent moments all he could do was stare.

Finally he lifted out a faded leather book and held it as gently as if holding a long-lost treasure. "Aunt Sarah's journal." He ran a hand over the cover, tracing the raised letters of his aunt's name. "It's been here all along."

As his astonishment gave way to a look of pure tenderness, Courtney felt tears well up and threaten to spill over. "You need some time alone to read this."

"No." He caught her hand. "Stay. We'll read it together."

She shook her head firmly. "Your aunt went to a lot of trouble to keep this hidden until you could uncover it. I need to drive over to The Willows, anyway. My family had invited me to dinner, and I'd begged off. This will give me the perfect opportunity to visit with them while you read your aunt's journal."

He gave her a quick, hard kiss. "An hour ought to be enough time. Then I'm going to start missing you."

She kissed him back. "You'd better miss me."

With a wave of her hand she turned away. At the door she turned back, but he was already settled into a chair and opening the first page.

He was so engrossed in the words, he didn't even hear her leave.

"Courtney." Trudy's smoke-roughened bark had her smiling before she even walked through the doorway. "You're in time for dessert. The folks are out on the patio. The mayor's with them."

"Thanks, Trudy. No dessert. I've already eaten. But I'll have some of that coffee I smell."

"You got it, honey." The housekeeper led the way toward the kitchen and paused to fill a steaming cup while Courtney continued to the patio.

"Poppie. Bert." She paused to kiss her grandparents. "Mayor Bentley." He stood and brushed a kiss over her cheek.

Courtney glanced around. "Where's Mom?"

"Working late." Frank patted the chair beside his. "She had a client flying in to go through the McShane estate."

Courtney sat beside her grandfather. "What brings you here tonight, Wade?"

"As I explained to your grandparents, I've made the decision to run for state senate, and I came seeking their endorsement."

"As if that would carry any weight," Frank said with a laugh.

"You're just being modest, Judge. You have a reputation for honesty and integrity that every politician in this state respects. Your endorsement would mean a lot to me."

Frank smiled. "Then you have it, Wade." He caught Courtney's hand. "Now tell me why my favorite granddaughter is here instead of out sailing on a night like this."

''No time for sailing tonight, Poppie. I had dinner with Blair Colby at his place.''

The old man glanced at his watch with a devilish grin. ''A bit early for the evening to end. Or did the two of you have some sort of spat?''

''Nothing of the sort.'' Courtney laughed. ''But the most amazing thing happened. We discovered his aunt's journal. All this time it had been hidden in plain sight.''

''I don't understand.'' Bert leaned close. ''Sarah Colby actually left a diary?''

''So it seems. A drawer in her desk had a false bottom. Underneath was an old leather book that seemed to have been written in her hand. I thought I'd leave Blair alone to read it.'' She turned to the mayor, who was listening in silence. ''You were right all along, Wade. Sarah left something, though whether it was a personal diary or a journal of the town's history, I can't say.''

''Just lying in her desk all these years, gathering dust,'' he said absently.

''Isn't that amazing?'' She turned to her grandfather. ''Would you mind if I invited Blair to brunch again tomorrow?''

''Of course I wouldn't mind.'' He patted her hand just as Trudy stepped onto the patio, rolling a serving cart laden with a silver coffee service.

While evening fell and the sky glittered with sparkling diamonds, they sipped their coffee and talked about Devil's Cove, its past and bright future. When the conversation turned to politics, Courtney got to her feet.

"It's time I got back." She kissed her grandparents and offered her hand to Wade Bentley. "Good luck on your campaign."

"Thank you." He turned to Frank. "I've taken up too much of your time, Judge. I think I should go, too."

"Not on your life." Frank Brennan chuckled. "Let's retire to my office, and you can tell me your campaign theme. Next to the law, there's nothing I like better than a stimulating political debate."

While Bert walked her granddaughter to her car, Frank and Wade stepped inside.

Bert chuckled in the gathering darkness. "Good. Now I can go upstairs and get lost in the romance I started reading earlier in the day."

Courtney looked surprised. "Bert, you always loved politics."

"And still do. But in this case, now that Wade has decided to run, it won't even be a contest. With his family name and excellent credentials,

all Wade has to do is get his name on the ballot
and he's assured of a win.''

"That's lucky for us, I suppose." Courtney
opened her car door. "At least we know we're
getting an honest man." She kissed her grandmother before settling herself inside and turning
the ignition. "See you at brunch."

When she returned to Blair's cottage, she found
him sitting exactly where she'd left him, the book
lying closed in his lap.

She tried to read his expression. He seemed
happy, sad, stunned.

She crossed the room and knelt beside him, taking his hands in hers. "Are you all right?"

"Yes. I'm…" He shook his head. "I'm not
sure yet how I feel. But I can tell you this. My
aunt Sarah had quite the story to tell."

"About herself? Or this town?"

"Both, I suppose." He smiled at her. "Did you
tell your grandparents about our discovery?"

"Yes. I hope you don't mind. And Wade Bentley was there, too. He's decided to run for state
senate and was seeking Poppie's endorsement.
Bert thinks this is just his first step toward the U.S.
Senate, and possibly higher."

At the crunch of tires on the driveway they both
looked up. At a knock on the door, Blair heaved

himself from the chair and crossed the room. When he opened the door, he gave a tired smile to his late-night caller.

"Mayor Bentley. Come in. I've been expecting you."

Chapter 15

Wade's eyes grew flinty. "What do you mean, you were expecting me?"

Behind Blair, Courtney wondered the same thing. But she was too surprised to say a word.

"When Court told me you were at The Willows and overheard the news of our discovery, I figured you wouldn't waste any time getting over here."

"Then I'm right to suspect that my family's name appears in your aunt's journal?"

Blair nodded. "Prominently."

"I want that book, Colby."

At the angry tone of his voice, Courtney opened

her mouth to protest. Before she could say a word Blair further confused her by handing the book over without a fight. "I want you to read it, Mayor Bentley."

Wade seemed startled. "You...don't object?"

"Not at all." Blair led him across the room and indicated the comfortable chair and table lamp. "Sit here. Courtney and I need some fresh air. When you're finished, we'll talk."

The mayor eyed him suspiciously. "What if I decide to destroy it while you're gone?"

Blair merely smiled. "I think, by the time you're finished, you'll change your mind. Or rather, Sarah will change it for you." He caught Courtney's hand and led her toward the door. "Make yourself comfortable, Mayor Bentley."

Courtney was too confused, her mind too befuddled, to do more than allow herself to be led in silence along the dock. When they came to the end, Blair sat down and she settled herself beside him.

When he dropped an arm around her shoulders, she turned worried eyes to him. "Was Wade the vandal?"

He nodded. "I'm pretty sure of it, though I'll want to hear it from his own lips."

"But why?"

"He believes there are things in Sarah's journal that will ruin his political career."

"Are there?"

Blair shrugged. "I suppose in the wrong hands it could prove damaging. But that isn't why my aunt wrote it. This isn't about revenge or ruining anyone's good name."

"Why did she write it?"

"She wanted to leave me something of herself. Something positive enough to undo some of the damage that had been done, I think."

"What kind of damage?" She touched a hand to his. "Blair, why have you never told me about yourself and your family?"

"Until now I thought only of the negatives. But after reading Sarah's journal, I can see that there were plenty of positives, as well. I just hadn't been aware of them."

When he saw the questions in Courtney's eyes he drew up one knee and wrapped his arms around it, staring at the path of moonlight across the water. "The first time I came here, I was a frightened, angry eight-year-old, whose parents had gone through a bitter divorce, leaving me to fend for myself while they continued to inflict as much damage on each other as was humanly possible.

When I first saw my aunt Sarah at the train station, I saw a cranky old spinster who welcomed me, not with open arms but with strict rules. At bedtime, instead of hugs and kisses, she read aloud to me from the classics until I fell asleep. As the years went by and my parents drifted from one messy relationship to another, my summers with my aunt were my only constant. Despite the lack of affection, there was a sort of permanence here. Her rules became part of my life, whether I liked them or not. Her discipline became mine. And, I suppose, her cold acceptance of the way things are seeped into my conscience. Because I preferred a life alone to one of constant tension, I decided that marriage wasn't in the stars for anyone with half a brain in the Colby family. We were a breed apart.''

"How has Sarah's journal changed that?"

Her question had him going very still. "I always thought of Sarah as a spinster because no man would have her. A tough old bird who had no patience for men or their weaknesses. What I learned from her letters is that she had, in fact, a wildly passionate love affair with a man. A married man. She had come here to Devil's Cove to consider his proposal. But when she saw what my parents' bitter divorce had done to me, she made a choice that would forever change not only her life but that of her lover. He had children, you see, and she couldn't bear the thought of inflicting the pain on them that she saw me endure.''

Courtney's eyes went wide. ''Wade's father?''

Blair nodded. ''She had been his secretary, and then his personal assistant. She describes in detail how it happened, gradually, over a period of years, until one day they could no longer deny the passion between them. When she ended it, he begged her to reconsider. She admits in her journal that forbidding him to ever see her or call her or write her was the hardest thing she'd ever done in her entire life. But she did it for me. For his own children. And, finally, for her own sense of self-worth. And she died without regrets.'' His voice lowered. ''What she wrote is a series of love letters to the nephew who, without ever being held or hugged by her, owned her heart. What she gave me is a renewed sense of respect for my family and for myself.'' He leaned toward Courtney and brushed her mouth with his. ''I have you to thank for discovering the hiding place of this extraordinary series of love letters.''

''You would have found her journal eventually.''

''Maybe. But I've opened that drawer a dozen

times or more since coming back, and never once did I think about the lack of depth." He chuckled. "And I call myself an architect. Scale should be one of the first things I notice."

"Hidden in plain sight."

He nodded. "Exactly. It was brilliant. But she was counting on my finding it eventually."

They both looked over when the door to the cottage opened and light spilled into the darkness. Seeing the mayor standing there, Blair caught Courtney's hand and led her along the dock to the porch.

Wade Bentley cleared his throat, and it was obvious that he'd been deeply moved by what he'd read. His earlier anger had drained away, leaving him close to tears.

"Come inside, Wade." Blair stepped past him and moved to the cupboard, where he removed a bottle of whiskey. "We need to talk."

While Blair filled three tumblers, and Courtney took a seat at the table, Wade paced back and forth, too agitated to sit.

"When did you first learn about your father and my aunt?" Blair asked as he offered Wade a drink.

"When my father knew he was dying. He told me there were things I ought to know." Wade drank half the liquid in one long swallow. "I was shocked. I'd always thought my parents had the world's perfect marriage. I remember being glad that my mother was already dead and wouldn't have to hear any of this garbage if it should find its way into the media." He lifted the tumbler and drained it. "Then I got angry. At my father. At your aunt. Especially your aunt, for telling my father she'd kept a journal, and was leaving it to her nephew. How dare she leave a smear on my family's good name!" His tone lowered. "It's been eating at me for years. And then, when your aunt died and I knew the cottage was vacant, I thought I'd search for the journal. All I wanted to do was destroy it so it wouldn't be around to dredge up old scandals."

"And possibly mar your political future?" Blair's voice was equally passionate.

"Yeah. There's that." Wade eyed the whiskey bottle, and Blair filled the tumbler a second time before handing it to him.

This time Wade took just a sip before sitting beside Courtney at the table. "I didn't mean to scare anyone. But after you moved in, I figured maybe you brought the journal with you, and I was desperate to find it and destroy it."

"That's how you happened to be here when the police came."

Wade nodded. "After taking the two of you out for coffee, I realized you'd never read the journal. I could tell you didn't have a clue about my father and your aunt."

Blair ran a finger around the rim of his untouched drink. "What did you think I'd do with the journal if I found it?"

"There are political enemies who would pay a lot of money to learn these secrets. I figured you'd use it to destroy me."

"Wouldn't I have to destroy my aunt's reputation in the process?"

Wade shrugged. "I guess I wasn't thinking about that. I just knew that whoever had your aunt's journal held my political future in their hands."

Blair looked directly at him. "I'm not interested in your future, Wade. Political or otherwise. As I told Courtney, I see my aunt's journal as a very personal love letter to me. But I do believe you owe it to the police chief, and to those who believe in your political future, to be honest and forthright about what you've done. You brought a sense of fear to this good community. You caused the police force to work overtime. And you're asking decent, trusting people to endorse you for high political office.''

Wade blanched. "You're right, of course. I'll talk to Chief Thompson first thing in the morning." He turned to Courtney. "I'll tell your grandfather what I did, and why, and place my future in his hands. That is, if I have any future left in politics.''

Courtney felt tears sting her eyes. "The worst thing you did was to plant the seed of mistrust about a sweet girl who works for me.''

"Kendra. I feel rotten about that." Leaving the rest of his drink untouched, he pushed away from the table. "I know an apology at this late date can't undo all the damage I've done. But believe me when I say how sorry I am about all of this.'' He turned to Blair. "Your aunt was a really special lady. It took real courage to face up to what she and my father had done, and from her journal, I know that she suffered terrible loneliness after cutting him out of her life. I'm glad she had you every summer.''

"I'm glad we had each other." Blair managed a smile as he accepted the mayor's handshake. "Thanks, Wade. Whatever you decide about your political future, I wish you luck.''

When the mayor was gone, Blair returned to the table and glanced at their untouched drinks.

Picking up his tumbler, he touched the rim of his glass to Courtney's. "To Aunt Sarah."

"To Aunt Sarah."

They drank and then, without a word, they stood and linked hands as they went about the room turning out the lights before making their way to the bedroom.

With only the spill of moonlight through the window, Blair gathered Courtney close and pressed his mouth to a tangle of hair at her temple.

His voice was hushed in the darkness. "I honestly thought there was a gene rendering our family incapable of love. I really believed that the only thing we could master was short-term relationships. It's why I never thought about my own future. Now I feel reborn. Thanks to Sarah, I realize that it's possible for even a Colby to demonstrate courageous, unselfish acts of love."

Slowly, softly, as though he had all the time in the world, he undressed her before moving to the bed where, with the softest of sighs and the gentlest of touches, he took her on a sweet, unhurried journey of love.

Epilogue

Courtney lay amid the twisted bed linens, gravitating toward the spill of sunlight through the gap in the curtains. As she shifted, she realized she was alone in bed.

She looked across the room to see Blair quietly turning the page of his aunt's journal. When he realized she was awake he looked over, and she felt a jolt at the look in his eyes. There was a calmness, a serenity, that she'd never seen before.

"'Morning, sleepyhead.'' He crossed the room to sit on the edge of the bed and brush her mouth with his.

Would she always feel this jolt at the mere touch of him? ''How long have you been awake?''

''Hours.'' He nodded toward the kitchen. ''I'll get you some coffee.''

She lay back, feeling pampered. His lovemaking during the night had been so tender, so careful, as though she were made of spun glass and he was afraid one wrong move might cause her to shatter. When had this careless, cocky bachelor become the ultimate lover?

''Here.'' He waited until she propped herself up with pillows before handing her a cup.

She sipped, and wondered at the lightness around her heart. ''Still reading your aunt's journal, I see.''

He nodded. ''I suppose each time I read it, I'll find something new that I overlooked before.'' He paused and chose his words carefully. ''I'd like you to read it when you have time.''

She couldn't think of a higher compliment. ''I'd love to, Blair.''

He brightened. ''Good. Maybe later today. Right now, I think we'd better get ready for brunch with your family.''

She laughed. ''I'm glad one of us has a brain this morning. I'd completely forgotten what day it is.''

* * *

Trudy looked up from the stove when Courtney and Blair stepped into the kitchen. "You missed the excitement."

"What excitement?" Courtney reached over the old housekeeper's shoulder and broke off a piece of cinnamon roll, only to have her knuckles rapped by a wooden spoon.

"No samples." Trudy stepped in front of the pan so Courtney couldn't reach for another taste. "The police chief was here with the mayor. They were closed in the Judge's office for an hour or more. When they came out, everybody looked pretty grim. If you ask me, I think they've figured out who those vandals were, but nobody's talking."

"Are they staying for brunch?" Courtney glanced out the French doors.

"Nope. The Judge invited them, but they said they had things to do." Trudy offered Blair her most inviting smile. "I guess since Courtney had a sample, I could give you one, too."

"Thanks, Trudy." He accepted the other half of the cinnamon roll and gave a sigh of pleasure. "I don't know how I'll ever be able to eat a store-bought roll again."

"Huh. Those things. Pure junk," she said with contempt. "You want real food, you just ask old Trudy."

He winked as he followed Courtney out to the patio.

As always, Frank Brennan stood by the grill, turning giant slabs of salmon, beef and sausage with one of his latest inventions, a combination spatula, fork and something that looked like a squeegee. Standing around him holding frosted drinks were Emily's husband, Jason Cooper, and Hannah's husband, Ethan Harrison.

The women were busy setting the table, arranging flowers and rolling out a serving tray on which rested a tray of assorted juices and a bottle of champagne.

While Courtney joined her mother, grandmother and sisters, she noted that Blair headed over to join the men. A short time later he and Frank disappeared inside the house, leaving Jason and Ethan to handle the grill.

When Blair and her grandfather emerged a short time later, they were talking and laughing together with the sort of camaraderie usually reserved for comfortable old friends. Though she wondered about it, Courtney had little time to think before being given the task of finding something heavy enough to anchor the pretty lace tablecloth that covered the patio table.

Bert pointed to the open doors. ''There are two crystal vases shaped like shells in the great room that would look perfect with Sidney's flower arrangement.''

Overhearing his wife, Frank turned to Blair. ''Maybe you'd better give Courtney a hand with those.''

Blair nodded and followed Courtney inside.

''I saw you talking with Poppie.'' Courtney found the shell vases and handed one to him. ''Did he tell you what the mayor and police chief had to say?''

''The mayor confessed to the vandalism and offered to withdraw his name from the ballot. For now he's in a sort of political limbo while the powers-that-be decide his future. Your grandfather said that after Chief Thompson thundered around the room for a while, he calmed down enough to admit that there wasn't anything he could do unless we swore out a warrant for the mayor's arrest. He'll be talking to us later today. I've already assured your grandfather that I don't want a pound of flesh. I'd just as soon see the issue fade away.''

Courtney touched a hand to his cheek. "You're a good man, Blair Colby."

He caught her wrist, stilling her movement. "Do you mean that?"

Her smile faded when she saw the intense look in his eyes. "Of course I mean it. Why do you ask?"

"Because you deserve a good man, Courtney. A man who'll never betray your trust. A man who'll stand beside you always, no matter what."

She started to draw back. "You're so serious, Blair, you're scaring me."

"Good. At least I have your attention."

"Of course you…" She stopped. Her smile returned. "You have my full and complete attention, Mr. Colby."

"Your grandfather and I didn't just come in here to talk about the mayor. I wanted to get him alone so I could ask his permission to marry his granddaughter."

When she merely stared at him, he grinned. "I see I've rendered you speechless. That's good, I think. Anyway, I asked your grandfather's blessing, and he gave it. So now…" He dropped to his knees and took her hands in his. "Courtney, will you marry me?"

She felt the quick rush of tears and blinked hard

to hold them back. The last thing she wanted was anything that would mar this moment.

Very slowly he stood and gathered her into his arms. "I never thought, when I was that angry little boy, that I'd want to spend my life in Devil's Cove. But meeting you changed everything. Here, with you, is the only place I want to be. I want to sail these waters with you, and walk these hills. I want to build my dream home here, somewhere nearby on the water, and grow old with you." He tipped up her chin and stared deeply into her eyes. "Please don't say no, Courtney. I can't imagine my life without you."

"Oh, Blair. How could I refuse you? I thought I would never trust a man again. But I'd trust you with my heart. My life. My future."

He brushed his mouth over hers. "Is that a yes?"

There was a distinct cough from the doorway, and they looked up to see her entire family standing behind her mother and grandparents. All of them grinning wildly.

"Was that a yes?" Frank Brennan demanded.

"Poppie. I can't believe you were eavesdropping."

"Not eavesdropping, my darling. Openly listening. This is, after all, our home. Now tell me what you said. We're waiting for your answer.''

She turned to Blair and brushed her mouth over his. ''Yes. Oh, yes, my darling. Yes.''

Frank cupped a hand to his ear. ''Eh? What did she say?''

''She said yes,'' came a chorus of voices behind him.

Ignoring their audience, Blair gathered her into his arms and kissed her thoroughly, much to the delighted cheers and shouts of her family.

Against his lips she whispered, ''You see what you're getting yourself into?''

''Pure heaven,'' he muttered. ''Wait until you meet my family.''

And then they found themselves being hustled out to the patio where they were toasted with champagne and orange juice and fed vast quantities of salmon and sausage and steak.

Across the patio Bert turned to her husband with tear-dampened lashes and kissed his cheek.

He touched a finger to the spot. ''What's that for?''

''For yesterday. For today. And for all our tomorrows. For starting this wonderful dynasty that brings us so much pleasure.''

''It's been quite a ride, hasn't it, love?'' He

followed the direction of her gaze and saw Courtney and Blair seated close together, their heads bent in quiet conversation. "Another love match."

"I wasn't expecting this one. I was afraid our girl had been too badly hurt."

He merely smiled. "Hearts can be mended. But only by love."

As they watched, the objects of their discussion laughed and held hands and knew that when this day ended, they would return to Blair's little cottage, where they would put aside the past and plan their future together.

Together.

The very thought had them turning to each other and smiling at the wonder of it all. Who would ever have believed that a man determined never to marry and a woman equally determined never to trust her heart to another man could find so much happiness?

In the midst of all the chatter Blair drew her close to brush his mouth over hers. "I love you, Courtney Brennan."

"And I love you, Blair Colby. For now. Forever."

"Forever is an awfully long time."

Courtney shook her head. "I'm thinking it's not nearly long enough."

He drew her close and whispered, "Let's go for a walk along the shore. We'll never be missed."

As Courtney looped her arm through his, he leaned close to whisper, "Besides, we need to plan our dream house. Your grandfather mentioned a piece of land for sale just down the road."

Courtney was laughing as she strode along by his side. "Leave it to Poppie to find a way to keep us all close."

"I like the way he thinks. In fact, I like everything about your family. I'm going to love being part of this big, noisy bunch."

"That's good, because there's no way out now, Colby."

He stopped and drew her close for a long, lingering kiss. "Promise?"

"You bet."

His grin was quick and dangerous. "I love you, Courtney Brennan. And I'm going to do everything in my power to prove it to you for the rest of our lives."

Courtney looked out over the tranquil waters of Lake Michigan and wondered at the lightness around her heart. A year ago she'd thought her heart was broken beyond repair. Yet here she was ready to trust again. This time, she knew, there was no risk involved. This time, the love was real. And her poor, shattered heart was whole and healed, thanks to the love of this very special man.

*   *   *   *   *

Look for RETRIBUTION,
the final book in the
Devil's Cove *series, featuring*
youngest sister Sidney Brennan,
coming in July 2004, only from
Silhouette Intimate Moments.
Turn the page
for a sneak preview...

Chapter 1

Devil's Cove—Present Day

"I know, Picasso. You're always in a hurry." Sidney looked over at the scrawny mutt with gray, wiry hair that made him look like a cross between a steel-wool scrubbing pad and a wire brush. She'd found him cowering in the woods the previous winter, and was delighted when her ad in the local newspaper had produced no one interested in claiming him, for the truth was, this poor, bedraggled little dog had stolen her heart. "Why can't you be serene, like Toulouse?"

The object of her praise, a black-and-white tabby that had wandered in several months ago and had made himself at home, was busy weaving circle eights between the dog's legs. Odd, Sidney thought, that these two different animals had formed an instant bond. As though each recognized in the other a kindred spirit. The lost and lonely, seeking love and the comfort of home, of someone to tend to their needs.

But while she was tending them, she realized they were filling a need in her, as well. They might be just two little animals, but they were someone to talk to in the silence of the day. Warm bodies in the darkness of the night. Boon companions to whom she could confide her most intimate secrets, without fear of ever having them revealed to others. Their companionship eased the enforced loneliness that had become a necessary part of her life.

"All right. I know it's time to go." With a sigh Sidney drained the last of her coffee and set the cup in the dishwasher before picking up her easel and canvas, a wooden case that held her paints and brushes, and a small folding stool. All of these were placed in an old wooden wagon.

The minute she opened the door, the dog and cat ran ahead, ready for another day of adventure.

"Oh sure. Once we're outside, you never wait for me." With a laugh she closed the door to the little cabin that she now called home.

When she'd first returned to Devil's Cove, she'd lived at The Willows, the lovely old mansion overlooking Lake Michigan that had been her family's home for more than fifty years. That was where her grandparents lived, and where her mother had first come as a bride, with her father. It was where they had raised their four daughters, and where each of Sidney's sisters had lived until finding a home of their own.

For the first few months Sidney had welcomed the tender ministrations of her family. The serene walks along the shore with Bert. The long, late-night talks with Poppie in his study. And the determination by Trudy, their lifelong house-keeper, to, as Trudy had said in that wonderful old rusty-gate voice, "ply her with food and put some weight on her bones." But before long Sidney had recognized the worried looks, the questioning glances that passed between her family members. Their constant hovering had begun to make her feel helpless, and more than a little smothered. Despite the fact that she was still grieving, and feeling confused about how to get on with her life, she recognized that it would be far too easy to become dependent upon her family for the strengths she needed to find within herself.

"Not yet, dear," Bert had said gently when Sidney first mentioned finding a place of her own. "It's too soon. Your emotions are still too raw. Let us indulge you a while longer."

"Besides," Poppie had said a bit more vehemently, "who would stay up late with me and argue the latest murder cases being aired on the news?"

"If you go," Trudy said in that raspy, rusty-nail voice roughened by years of smoking, "your grandfather will be forced to eat an entire batch of chocolate-chip cookies by himself. And then his cholesterol will go up, and his blood pressure, and who knows what else?"

Sidney had remained adamant. "I won't be bribed or made to feel guilty about going. It's time."

Once she'd begun seriously shopping for a place to call her own, her mother, Charley, a real estate agent, had discovered this little cabin in the woods. From the moment Sidney set foot inside, she'd known it was meant to be.

She still felt a thrill each time she returned home. She loved everything about it. The way it sat, snug and perfect amid the towering pines that surrounded it. The way the waters of Lake Michigan, shimmering just a stone's throw away, beckoned. The cozy feeling of the cedar logs that formed the walls, and the high, natural wood beams framing skylights that allowed light to stream in even on the grayest of days. Though it was small, with just a single bedroom, a great room and galley kitchen, it was more than enough space for her. She'd turned the upper loft into her studio where she could happily lose herself in her work, when the weather wouldn't permit her to paint outside. Despite the unreliable Michigan weather and its often turbulent storms, Sidney much preferred to paint in the open air, by the water's edge, rather than paint her subjects from memory. There was just something about the antics of the waterfowl that were her specialty that could always be counted on to make her smile. The ducks, the geese, the herons that fished these waters were natural clowns, causing no end of amusement. Best of all, they seemed undisturbed by her presence. Because they'd become accustomed to her sitting at her easel along the shore, they went about their business without distraction.

With the dog and cat sniffing a hundred scents in the forest, Sidney pulled the loaded wagon along the trail through the woods until she emerged in bright sunlight at the water's edge. This was one of her favorite spots. It took only minutes to set up her equipment. Then, after watching a family of ducks splashing near shore, beside a half-submerged wooden rowboat that had stood along the shore for years, she picked up her brush and began to bring them to life on her canvas.

Adam Morgan sat straight up in bed, ready to bolt, when he came fully awake and realized he'd been in the throes of the recurring nightmare. Rubbing a hand over his face, it took him a moment to gather his thoughts. The doctors had warned him that these terrifying dreams were part of the healing process. Though the wounds to his body were visible, and therefore easier to tend, the ones in his mind were no less serious. There were too many things about the incident that were still lost to his conscious memory. But they were there, locked away in his mind, and when he relaxed in sleep, they rose to the surface, taunting him with bits and pieces of the terror he'd experienced. There was still so much about the accident that he couldn't remember. But he'd been assured by his doctors that it would all come back to him in time.

He slid out of bed and moved slowly across the room. Filling a glass with water, he gulped down two capsules, then leaned on the bathroom sink and waited for the dizziness to pass. He caught a glimpse of himself in the mirror and winced. Eyes bloodshot. Cheeks and chin darkened by several days' growth of beard. It would take too much energy to shave. Besides, why bother? Who would see him here, in the middle of nowhere?

The doctors had done all they could. Now, they warned him, what he most needed was time. His frown deepened. Time. There would be plenty of that now. He couldn't return to work until the madman who dogged his trail was captured and put away for good. Twice Adam had managed to elude his stalker, and twice the man had proved just as adept at escaping the authorities, despite their best efforts.

It had been Phil Larken, Adam's boss and president of WNN, World News Network, who had arranged for Adam to use this lighthouse as his own private retreat. Though the nearby town of Devil's Cove was small, there was a modern medical clinic, and an excellent physical therapist. Since Adam couldn't return to work until he had a clean bill of health from the doctors, and since they weren't about to let him off the hook until he'd completed at least six months of therapy for the shoulder that had been shattered in the blast, this place afforded him the perfect refuge until he could take back his life.

Odd, he thought as he returned to the bedroom. He'd been working nonstop since his college days. He couldn't remember the last time he'd taken time off. As a photojournalist for World News Network, he'd covered every hot spot in the world. Asia, Africa, Europe, the Middle East. How ironic that his injuries had occurred, not in some troubled corner of the world, but right here in the United States, in New York City, outside the United Nations Building.

Now, here he was, feeling as though he'd been caught in a time-warp. He looked around as though still doubting he was really here. The last time he'd been in Devil's Cove, he'd been all of twelve, on a fishing trip with his uncle. He'd taken one look at the lighthouse that sat on a finger of land that jutted into Lake Michigan and fell wildly, madly in love. There was just something about the look of it. That tall spire looking out over miles and miles of nothing but dark water, its beacon the only warning the captain and crew of ships plying this lake had of the dangerous shoals and shallows that lurked beneath the waves.

And now it was his home. At least until he healed. And all because, in a moment of dark depression, he'd confided in Phil that if he had to do nothing for six months, he'd surely go crazy. When Phil asked if there was any place he might be able to endure the boredom, Adam had blurted out his boyhood fascination with the lighthouse. The next thing he knew, Phil had used his considerable influence to make it happen. Adam had been invited by the historical society to spend the off-season living in the Devil's Cove Lighthouse, in exchange for photographing the various changes of season for their almanac. Simple work. A simple lifestyle. And because it had all been arranged quickly, and in complete privacy, the authorities were hoping that this time, his stalker would be confounded. Not that Adam believed it was over and he was safe. He'd believe that only when the assassin who'd triggered the car bomb that killed the ambassador and his assistant was behind bars, and not a minute sooner.

Moving like a slug he climbed the dozens of stairs that led to the tower. Though the ships passing through the Great Lakes had long ago switched to the latest in high-tech navigational equipment, and the lighthouse was no longer necessary to the boaters' safety, the computer-operated light still went on every day at dusk and stayed on until morning. There was something comforting in that. The sameness of it gave him a sense that, in a world gone crazy, some things never changed.

When he reached the top he looked down at the serene waters, reflecting the forest that ringed its banks, alive with fiery autumn foliage. Smoke drifted from an ore carrier moving slowly up-river. In the distance was a ship bearing a foreign flag. Several sailboats danced across the waves, and Adam wondered at the hardy souls willing to risk the wrath of frigid water and fickle winds. Still, if he had the strength, he knew he'd be out there with them. Hadn't he always enjoyed a challenge? It was one of the reasons he thrived on the dangers of his job.

He walked over to the telescope he'd set up, so that he could keep a close eye on his surroundings. Peering through the lens he stared around, thinking there couldn't be a more beautiful place in the world than Michigan in fall. Especially here on the shore of Lake Michigan. As long as he had to spend his sick leave somewhere private, there wasn't anywhere he could think of that would suit him more, so long as he could see an end to the idyll. He knew himself well enough to be certain that even paradise would seem like a prison to him if it stretched on endlessly. He was determined to get out of here as soon as the doctor's projected goal of six months of therapy was over. He shook his head, trying to recall the last time he'd spent six months in one place.

Now that the daylight was fading to dusk, he decided to grab a camera and try for a few shots of the nearby forest at sunset. If nothing else, it would take his mind off his pain and boredom.

Sidney alternately watched the antics of the duck family, and lowered her head to return her attention to her canvas, perfectly capturing the line, the form, the symmetry of each of her models.

In early spring she'd watched this pair of proud mallards bring their six babies to the water and hover over them as they'd taken their first swim near shore. Now the six were as big as their parents, and ready for the flight south with other migrating flocks. To prepare for the grueling trip, they were driven to search out as much food as their bodies could hold. Tipping upside down to feed on the bottom of the shallows, only their tail feathers were visible. It was a sight she always found endearing. She'd already thought of the title for the painting. *Bottom's Up*. That had her grinning.

Though the earlier afternoon sunshine had caused her to discard her corduroy jacket and roll up her sleeves, she now shivered in the gathering shadows as she struggled to put this entire scene on canvas before the duck family decided to depart for warmer climates.

Picasso lay at her feet, panting from his romp in the woods, his fur matted with burrs that would take most of the evening to remove. Toulouse was nowhere to be seen, but Sidney wasn't worried. Even if he stayed out all day, stalking field mice, that cat was smart enough to show up at her door in time for dinner. Toulouse never missed a meal or a chance to curl up before the fire.

She added a dab of paint to her palette, mixed it, and bent to her work.

Picasso's ears lifted. He sprang to his feet, a low warning growl issuing from his throat.

Surprised, Sidney turned in time to see a shadow emerging from the cover of the woods. As the shadow separated itself from the others, she realized it was a man. At first, judging by his rough beard and even rougher garb, she thought he might be a hunter, until she realized that he was carrying, not a rifle, but a camera. A second camera hung from a strap around his neck.

He paused, allowing the dog to get close enough to take his scent.

"Sorry. Didn't mean to startle you." His voice was deep, the words spoken abruptly, as though he resented having to speak at all.

Sidney set aside her brush and wiped her hands on a rag before getting to her feet. "We don't see too many people out here."

"I didn't expect to run into anybody." He glanced around. "I don't see a car or a boat. How'd you get here?"

"I live over there." She pointed to the forest at his back.

"In those woods?" He shot her a look of surprise. "I was told this was federally protected land."

"It is. Or at least most of it is. My property was grandfathered in before the government bought the surrounding land. It's been owned by the same family since the turn of the century, so it remained private property. When it went on the market, I liked the idea of a guarantee that there would never be any neighbors."

She could feel him studying her a little too

intensely. When an uncomfortable silence
stretched between them she tried a smile. "How
about you? I don't believe I've seen you around
Devil's Cove before."

He didn't return the smile. "Just moved in."
He watched the way the dog moved to stand
protectively beside Sidney. "I'm staying in the
lighthouse."

"Really?" She turned to study the tower that
could be seen above the tree line. "How did you
manage that? I thought it was a historic building
now, and off-limits to the public."

"Just lucky, I guess. The historical society
asked me to photograph the area for their almanac.
In exchange, I get to stay there until next spring."

"Then you're a professional photographer?"

"Yeah." He glanced at the canvas. "And from
the look of that, I'd guess I'm in the company of
a professional artist."

When he made no move to introduce himself,
Sidney offered her hand. "I'm Sidney Brennan."

He seemed to pause a beat before saying
gruffly, "I think I've seen some of your work.
Wildlife?"

She nodded.

"Adam Morgan."

He had a strong, firm handshake, she noted, and

his eyes stayed steady on hers until she withdrew her hand and motioned toward the dog at her feet. "This is Picasso."

When he looked down the dog cocked his head to one side and regarded him. "A good watchdog."

She laughed. "He knows who feeds him."

"Lucky dog. Since I have to feed myself, I'm about to head back and see about dinner."

"Dinner?" Sidney glanced up at the sky, noting for the first time that the sun had begun to slip below the horizon. "I had no idea it was so late."

"That must mean you were having a good day."

She nodded, surprised that he understood. "That's right. I get so lost in my work, I forget everything. I even forget to eat."

"Yeah. I know the feeling." He turned toward the lighthouse in the distance. "Good night."

"Nice to meet you, Adam. Maybe I'll see you again sometime." Sidney began to pack up her paints.

Seeing her folding up her easel and camp stool, and packing them in the wagon, he paused, taking her measure. She was no bigger than a minnow, and couldn't weigh a hundred pounds. "You sure you can handle all that?"

"Don't worry. I haul it all the time."

She'd gone only a few paces when he fell into step beside her.

At her arched brow he merely took the handle from her hands. "Sorry. I've forgotten my manners. Living alone does that. I'd feel a lot better if you'd let me pull this."

It was on the tip of her tongue to refuse. She didn't know this man, and wasn't sure she wanted to get to know him. But she was feeling the effects of working all day without eating. Not really weak so much as light-headed. The thought of having help hauling this equipment home was comforting. "Thanks."

As they followed the path deeper into the woods, Sidney looked up at the canopy of fiery autumn foliage. "You picked a great time of year to visit."

When he didn't reply she added, "This is my favorite season."

"For the color?"

"There's that, of course. But it's more. The tourists are gone, a lot of the trendy shops are closed until next summer, and there's this wonderful feeling of anticipation."

He turned to her. "What is it you're anticipating?"

She shrugged. "Slowing down, I guess. Settling in for the winter. Have you ever spent a winter in Michigan?"

"No. Tell me what I'm in for."

She laughed. "Snow. Mountains of it. I hope you like skiing, sledding and ice fishing."

"I'll let you know after I've tried my hand at all of them."

"Where are you from?"

Again that pause, as though reluctant to reveal anything about himself. "Florida, originally. But it's been years since I've been back."

"Where do you live when you're not here, photographing nature?"

"Wherever an assignment takes me."

"Assignment?"

"I'm a photojournalist with WNN."

Her eyes widened. "Really? I've never met anyone who actually worked for television news before. I suppose you've been all over the world."

He merely gave a shrug of his shoulders, as though reluctant to talk about his work. And though it was on the tip of her tongue to ask why he was here in Devil's Cove, instead of some exotic location, there was something about his closed, shuttered look that told her he wouldn't be comfortable answering any more of her questions.

They came up over a rise and Adam stopped dead in his tracks at the sight of the cabin. "Talk about isolation."

Sidney couldn't decide if he was impressed or dismayed. "I guess I'm just comfortable with my own company. I knew, the minute I saw it, that it had to be mine."

He shot her a sideways glance as she opened the door and held it while he stepped past her. Once inside he handed her the easel and stool and she set them in a corner of the room, along with her paints and canvas.

When she turned, she saw him rubbing his shoulder. "Are you all right?"

"Yeah." He lowered his hand. "Just nursing an injury."

"You should have told me."

He shook his head. "Nothing to worry about. I'm fine."

Sensing that he was uncomfortable talking about it, she quickly changed the subject. "How about some cider before you go?"

"Cider?"

"Don't tell me you've never tried our Michigan cider?" Sidney opened the refrigerator and removed a jug. "Apple cider. Made just outside of town at the Devil's Cove Orchard and Old

Mill.'' She nodded toward the great room. ''Make yourself comfortable. I'll bring you a mug. You're in for a treat.''

''I'll stay here.'' He remained by the door. ''My boots would track dirt on your floor.''

''You could take them off.''

''I'd rather not.''

When he didn't move, Sidney filled two mugs with cider and handed him one before crossing to the fireplace, where she held a match to kindling. Within minutes a cozy fire was burning on the hearth.

She looked at the window with a laugh. ''I see Toulouse is back.''

While Adam watched with interest, she walked over, reached around him and opened the door. The black-and-white cat bounded inside and crossed the room to settle on a rug in front of the fire, where he began grooming himself.

''Another one of yours?'' Adam asked.

She nodded. ''Toulouse found us about six months ago. Just wandered in and never left.''

''Smart cat.'' Adam sipped his cider and looked around the cozy cabin, letting the warmth of the fire soothe his aching shoulder. The place smelled of cedar, of apples, and faintly of linseed oil. A bowl of apples adorned the coffee table set in front of the sofa. He looked up, admiring the rugged cedar beams overhead. Spying the loft he tilted his head for a better look. ''Your studio?''

''Yes. It's perfect under the skylights. I usually work there only when I can't paint outside. But I much prefer working in the fresh air, with my models posing in the water close to shore.''

''Models?''

She laughed. ''Ducks. Geese. All kinds of waterfowl. They're my specialty.''

''I see.'' He noted the number of canvases, stacked in no apparent order along the wooden railing, and the easel, positioned directly under the skylights. ''I guess I'll need some models, too. Deer and foxes, and whatever else I can scare up in these woods.''

''You'll be amazed at how much wildlife you'll see. This forest is alive with some wonderful creatures.''

He heard the warmth in her tone. ''I'm counting on it. I'm hoping to put together a workable darkroom at the lighthouse, so I won't have to send my work to an outside lab. There's a fairly good sized utility room on the lower level that I think might work. It has a small sink, and several long cabinets connected by a counter top. I think it'll give me the room I need to develop my prints.''

It was, Sidney realized, the most he'd said since they'd met. "It's so nice to be able to work at home. If you're like me, you're going to like living and working in the same space." She settled herself on the raised hearth and absently ran a hand over Toulouse's back. The cat closed his eyes and purred contentedly.

"Yeah, there's something to be said for that." Adam found himself watching the cat with envy. Sometimes, when Marcella Trowbridge, his physical therapist, whom he'd silently dubbed The Dominatrix, was pushing him to the limits of endurance, he wanted to ask her to stop and just massage his shoulder instead. Of course, Marcella wasn't being paid to soothe him. Her job was to get him back to normal, or as close to normal as possible, in the shortest amount of time. And she did that by beating him up on a regular basis, until he wanted to beg for mercy. Each time their therapy session ended, he felt like a whipped dog. He was intelligent enough to know it was necessary, and that it was, indeed, getting the job done. Without the therapy, he'd never be allowed back to work. But he couldn't help wishing for it to be over sooner rather than later.

To keep from thinking about what it would be like to be the one getting a back rub he turned his attention to the rest of the room. The walls were hung with paintings of waterfowl. Some were sweet. Families of ducks or geese swimming in perfect formation, mother in front, young in the middle, the father taking up the rear, head lifted to guard against predators. Some were poignant, like the one of a pair of ducks anxiously guiding their lone baby into the water for a first swim.

He stepped closer, careful to keep his muddy boots on the small square of rug at the door. "Those are wonderful. Are you able to make a living with your art?"

Sidney nodded. "I consider myself lucky. Several galleries carry my work. And since my sister Courtney came back to Devil's Cove and opened her shop, I haven't been able to keep up with the demand." She laughed. "My grandfather likes to say that Courtney could sell sand in the desert."

"I know the kind. A real people person. But I'm betting she doesn't have to twist any arms to sell this. You have an amazing talent."

"Thank you." She heard the wind pick up outside, and glanced at the window where red-and-gold leaves tumbled in a wild dance. The air had grown considerably colder now that the sun had set. On impulse she said, "I'm thinking of making an omelette for dinner. Would you like to stay?"

He gave a quick shake of his head and drained his mug before setting it on the kitchen table. "Sorry. I've got to go. But you were right. The cider was great."

"I thought you'd like it."

That wasn't all he liked. If he didn't know better, he'd think he'd just stumbled into some sort of enchanted cottage. And the red-haired woman with the soft green eyes was either a witch or a goddess.

He resolutely turned the knob and pulled open the door, absorbing a blast of chilly wind. "Good night."

Sidney hurried across the room and stood in the doorway, the dog and cat at her feet. "Good night, Adam. Maybe I'll see you again sometime."

Not likely, he thought as he started toward the beacon of light in the distance. The last thing he needed was a female cluttering up his already messed up life. Especially one that smelled of evergreen and had hair the color of autumn leaves, not to mention eyes all soft and deep and green. Eyes that a man could drown in.

He'd already made up his mind to carefully keep his distance from Sidney Brennan.

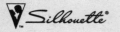

From the *USA TODAY* bestselling author of
Whiskey Island, Emilie Richards continues
her unforgettable tale of star-crossed lovers,
murder and three sisters who discover a hidden
legacy that will lead them home at last to Ireland.

"Emilie Richards presents us with a powerfully told story that
will linger in the heart long after the final page."
—*Book Page*

EMILIE
RICHARDS

THE
PARTING
GLASS

*Available in
June 2004
wherever
paperbacks
are sold.*

MIRA®

USA TODAY bestselling author

E R I C A
SPINDLER

Jane Killian has everything to live for. She's the toast of the Dallas art
community, she and her husband, Ian, are completely in love—and
overjoyed that Jane is pregnant.

Then her happiness shatters as her husband becomes the prime
suspect in a murder investigation. Only Jane knows better. She
knows that this is the work of the same man who stole her sense
of security seventeen years ago, and now he's found her again…
and he won't rest until he can *See Jane Die*…

SEE JANE DIE

"Creepy and compelling, *In Silence* is a real page-turner."
—*New Orleans Times-Picayune*

Available in June 2004 wherever books are sold.